#12498 M [illegible] $8.00 1929

MW01142081

THE CORDS
OF VANITY

Other Miles Tripp books published by St. Martin's

THE CORDS OF VANITY

Miles Tripp

Woe unto them that draw
iniquity with cords of vanity.

Isaiah, ch. 5, v. 18

ST. MARTIN'S PRESS
NEW YORK

Library of Congress Cataloging-in-Publication Data

Tripp, Miles,
        The cords of vanity / Miles Tripp.
                p.   cm.
        "A Thomas Dunne book."
        ISBN 0-312-04279-5 :
        I. Title.
PR6070.R48C67   1990
823'.914—dc20   89-78028
                                                              CIP

First published in Great Britain by Macmillan London Ltd.

First U.S. Edition

10 9 8 7 6 5 4 3 2 1

THE CORDS
OF VANITY

Chapter 1

The month was April but in south London it might still have been January. In the district where Samson had his office the only nesting bird was a lone pigeon trying to establish new quarters under the eaves of a vacant building on the opposite side of a busy street which was filled with slow-moving cars and pedestrians from every ethnic minority.

He paused from dictating a confidential report on the private life of a young man whose ambition was to be a captain of industry. The central heating had broken down and Samson was wearing an overcoat to keep warm. As he rubbed his hands together to stimulate circulation he watched the pigeon carrying a straw and felt sympathetic towards the bird. An epidemic of vandalism, the mugging of his secretary, Shandy, after she had left the office late one night, the lack of heating and a mounting spirit of restlessness had combined to make him dissatisfied with the location of his business premises. It was time to make a move.

A knock on his door and Shandy entered.

'There's a Mrs Huntingdon-Winstanley on the line. When I asked if I could help she told me to put her direct through to you. She doesn't discuss her affairs with floozies, acolytes or other hangers-on. And would I make it snappy. She hasn't got all day.'

'Put her through,' said Samson. 'She's obviously warmed you up. Maybe she could do the same for me.'

Mrs Huntingdon-Winstanley's voice was deep and strident. 'Mr Samson, I want your assistance. I should like to see you at once. At my residence. Have you a pencil handy? I'll give you my address.'

'You want my assistance? What sort of assistance?'

'I'm not prepared to say. As I've already told the girl who answered this call, I don't discuss my affairs with a total stranger on the telephone.'

'Understandably,' said Samson. 'Affairs are very private and confidential matters. Emotionally traumatic. I simply wanted to know what sort of assistance you needed.'

He heard a sharp intake of breath, and then, 'Will you, or will you not, come and see me?'

'Do you want the assistance of a private investigator and are you willing to pay an excessive fee for a visit?'

'Yes, yes, yes.'

'Then give me your address.'

As soon as he had replaced the handset Shandy poked her head round the door. 'I heard all that,' she said. 'She didn't like the bit about affairs.'

'People who dish it out should be prepared to take it,' he replied. 'I've been thinking. How would you feel if we moved office?'

'You've been talking about it for ages. I'd love it if the new place had a loo of its own. I'm fed up with sharing a loo with the Kirmani family. It's always occupied.'

Samson smiled. 'It must be Mrs Kirmani's curries. See you later.'

Mrs Huntingdon-Winstanley occupied the top two floors of a block of luxury apartments overlooking Regent's Park.

A maid, dressed in cap and apron, opened the door. She was a tiny middle-aged woman and she wore black rimmed spectacles.

'Samson,' said Samson.

8

'Yes, we have already been advised, sir. Please come in.' He was taken through a hall lined with mirrors to a large drawing room which was dominated by portraits of sullenly self-important figures from the eighteenth and nineteenth centuries. Some of the furniture was by Sheraton but delicate curves were concealed by carelessly draped fur stoles. A *chaise-longue* was swathed in an enormous coat of Russian sable. In the centre of the room an inlaid walnut table with fluted legs had four chairs placed around it. A pack of playing cards and a pile of small ivory ornaments lay on the table-top.

The maid left the room and Samson walked over to a bookcase. He believed that collected books revealed something of their collector. Many of the volumes on display were bound in tooled leather and blocked with gilt. The first titles he read were, *A Romantic Elopement*, *The Passionate Heart*, and *The Doctor who Loved too Much*. Much of the romantic fiction was by Ruby M. Ayres and Ethel M. Dell and these novels occupied one side of the bookcase. The other side contained books of a different genre. These were classics of French literature. Samson extracted a copy of *Eugénie Grandet* and found it was a French edition. *L'Avare* was also in French. If the books were representative of his potential client's tastes she liked English romantic fiction and French classics in the original version.

He had just put away Voltaire's *Dictionnaire philosophique* when the door opened and a deep voice said, 'Mr Samson?'

He turned and saw a woman who held herself regally erect, and he was reminded of pictures he had seen of Queen Mary, wife of George V, except that whereas the queen might have had a toque on her head Mrs Huntingdon-Winstanley was hatless. Her hair, of an unusual henna-chestnut colour, had silver highlights. The skin on her face might once have been fine but was now obscured by an incrustation of powder and two bright

rouge marks on her cheeks. Lipstick which matched her
long crimson velveteen gown couldn't conceal the thinness
of her lips. Her light blue eyes were lively and Samson
guessed she had once been beautiful. She was an amalgam
of superannuated madame and dowager duchess.

She hobbled forward using a walking stick more like
a scanning geiger counter than a support, and she held a
Gucci handbag. 'Do sit down,' she said, indicating a place
at the table.

'Here?' he enquired.

'Where else? You are here for business, not to lounge
about.'

In moving towards the table Samson barked his shin
on an unnoticed footstool. As he regained his balance Mrs
Huntingdon-Winstanley offered her stick. 'You look as if
you need this more than I.'

He gave her a wincing smile. 'I'm all right,' he said.
His clumsiness had been the result of not looking where
he was going because he had been reaching inside his coat
to switch on a miniaturised tape-recorder, and this covert
act had distracted his attention.

'I wish I was all right,' she said. 'I'm cursed with arthritis. Most incommoding . . . Can you play Spillikins, Mr
Samson?'

'Is it a game?'

'Yes. In America they call the game Jackstraws. A rather
plebeian word, don't you think? But just what one would
expect from a country which values democracy more than
aristocracy.' She indicated the pile of tiny ivory ornaments.
'We take it in turns to lift pieces but you mustn't disturb
the rest of the pile. If you do, you lose a point. We use
these.' She picked up a long needle-like stick of ivory
which had an exquisitely carved stem. 'It requires great
delicacy of touch,' she said. 'Do you have delicacy of
touch?'

Samson, whose big body, heavy head and short legs

10

could in surreal art have been depicted as a human hippopotamus, had small hands and feet. For a solidly built man he could be very nimble although the accident with the footstool had made him seem ungainly. He looked at his hands. 'Do I have delicacy of touch?' he mused. 'That's a question I've never been asked before and modesty would forbid me to answer.'

'Let's test you out then,' she said as she sat down at the opposite side of the table. 'Here you are.' She handed him an ivory stick. 'You will see that each of the pieces has a small hole in it and you use the stick to lift a spillikin out by its hole, but you must not disturb the other pieces. Is that clear?'

'Perfectly clear. What isn't clear is why you sent for me. I'm a private investigator not a professional playmate.'

Her crimson lips parted in a slight smile. 'I know exactly what you are. Now pay attention to the game. It's gone out of fashion in recent times. It was very popular in Victoria's reign. I'd like to rekindle interest. My company has been producing gold trinkets precisely modelled on these pieces. The pieces can either be used to play Spillikins which we shall try to popularise by advertising, or they can be threaded on a filigree gold chain and worn on the wrist, or, if one is a common woman, they can be worn round the ankle.'

Under his heavily lidded eyes Samson regarded her quizzically. 'You think it would catch on?'

'Certainly. What woman wouldn't want to play if she thought she was going to keep any winnings.'

Samson looked at the pieces which included among other items a tiny bell, a shoe and a cricket bat. He toyed with the ivory stick. 'Is that why I'm here? You're market-researching for ornamental bracelets and you want my opinion?'

'Don't be absurd. Shall I start?' She reached out an arthritic hand, trembling slightly, and managed to hook a tiny spade and place it on the table. 'Now it's your turn.'

Samson hadn't expected to find himself playing an obscure parlour game with a rich old lady but she had succeeded in arousing his curiosity and, as he had once explained to Shandy, 'Curiosity aids my investigative powers in the same way that a fine malt whisky aids my digestion.'

He poked with his stick at something resembling a crochet hook and the pile of ornaments was disturbed.

'One down to you, one up to me,' said Mrs Huntingdon-Winstanley with satisfaction. 'When you've got the hang of the game we might play for small stakes.'

As she probed for the replica of a throne Samson asked, 'Was I recommended to you or did you pick out my name at random from the Yellow Pages with a spillikin?'

'You were recommended.' The throne trembled slightly but she lifted it clear.

'I see. Someone who knew of my skill at Trivial Pursuit mentioned my name.'

She gave him an amused look. 'You are a droll fellow. No, the game was Hunt the Slipper.'

It took him almost five seconds to make the correct connection and, when he did, he thought, this eccentric old bird can play more than one game. He said, 'I played Hunt the Slipper, or Hunt the Shoe Fetishist, in Marseilles. Am I on the right lines?'

'You are.'

'Then I was recommended by Mr or Mrs Ormerod.'

'Correct. I met Mrs Ormerod some years ago at the home of a mutual friend. Although we've rather lost touch since the onset of my disability we speak occasionally on the telephone. I'm a great fan of her novels. She writes as Karen Fitzgerald.'

'I know. But I hadn't noticed any of her books on the shelves over there.' Samson glanced towards the bookcase.

12

'No. Those books are by 1920s writers. Karen and Cartland are in another room.'

Samson concentrated on picking up a minute penknife which had been so meticulously crafted that two tiny blades could be opened. When the penknife was clear he said, 'But you don't want me for Hunt the Slipper, or for this game we're playing. So what pastime do you have in mind?'

She put down her ivory stick. 'All right. Down to business. You've passed the test. Some delicacy of touch – the penknife is one of the most difficult – and you were quick enough in making the slipper connection. I want you to play Watch the Wandering Animal.'

'I don't know that game.'

'Then I'll explain. I have an animal which I don't want stolen. I want you to keep watch over it.'

In a thought process which would have matched a computer for speed Samson made connection between Karen Ormerod (or Fitzgerald) whom he had helped in Marseilles and rare animals trapped by her friend Paul Phelan, and concluded that Mrs Huntingdon-Winstanley might own a private zoo which held a rare animal, a giant panda perhaps, and she wanted him to make security arrangements. 'Is this animal valuable?' he asked.

'Would you call a goat valuable?'

'You want me to keep watch on a goat?'

'I want to know what the goat gets up to when it strays.'

Samson believed that strange whims, usually the product of some emotional or psychological driving force, could become distorted and fixed as an obsession, but an obsessive interest in a goat was something new to him. He glanced at the furs scattered around; none were of goatskin. Perhaps the peculiar old woman was playing a different sort of game; a game within a game of which only she knew the rules.

He leaned back and fixed his gaze at a late eighteenth-century crystal chandelier. 'Goat,' he mused aloud. 'I'm not sure of its genus, family or order, but its class is certainly mammalia. Now then, what science would be concerned with watching such a creature?' He closed his eyes in thoughtful concentration. 'An ethologist,' he exclaimed. 'Ethologists specialise in observing animal behaviour. I once read a book by a chap who was a devout watcher of the Uganda cob and there was another fellow who was marvellous at watching greylag geese. Who, I wonder, is the ethological expert on goat-watching?'

He opened his eyes. Mrs Huntingdon-Winstanley's face was cracked with lines of hauteur. 'Don't try to be funny at my expense, Mr Samson.'

Samson pushed his spillikin stick to one side. The time for games was over. 'I'm glad you mentioned expense,' he said. 'My services are very expensive; my fees higher than anyone else in my profession. When it comes to over-pricing I am an Olympic gold medallist. My fee for watching a goat would be very high indeed.'

She put down her spillikin stick, an acknowledgement that parlour games were finished and any battle was a battle of wits. 'Are you married, Mr Samson?' she asked.

He shifted in his seat. He disliked any enquiry into his private life although in his profession he enquired into the private lives of others. He had no intention of answering her question but it had given him the opening he needed. She had mentioned marriage immediately after he had referred to his fees. The two themes were probably linked. He nodded his head like a man who knows the answer to a conundrum before it has been half put to him. 'I see,' he said, 'you've asked me here today to discuss a matter connected with someone's marriage.'

A twinkle came to her bright blue eyes. 'Correct. And the someone is I. It is my marriage.'

Although the tape-recorder would provide a record of the interview he produced a notepad and ballpoint pen with the air of someone who doesn't allow a business opportunity to slip. He looked at her enquiringly. 'Your marriage, Mrs Hungtingdon-Winstanley?'

Speaking each word clearly she replied, 'I am married to a goat.'

On his notepad Samson wrote, 'Mrs H-W m. to goat.' He looked across the table at her. 'What is your husband's name? Pan?'

'Ha!'

He wasn't certain whether her exclamation was of anger or approval. Then she smiled. 'It should have been Pan, but his first name is Simon.'

'And he has a penchant for extra-marital affairs?'

A flicker of distaste crossed her face. 'Much as I dislike having to confide a private matter to a stranger I need your services, or the services of someone in your trade. There's no point in beating about the bush. Yes, he does have amours, but he has to be careful. You see, I hold the purse strings . . . ' She hesitated, 'At least, I think I do. I'm not so sure now.' She paused. 'Not so sure,' she repeated.

'You want me to find out whether he has another source of income?' Samson asked.

She didn't immediately answer his question. 'Until I was crippled by arthritis,' she said, 'I made sure things never got out of hand but now . . . He's sixty-five but thinks he's still forty and handsome.' Her lips thinned to a crimson thread. 'Unfortunately he isn't bad looking. It's quite unfair how some men can keep their looks. But I mustn't digress. Pan, did you say? More like an ageing Peter Pan than the Greek god. I'm sure tarts play him for what they can get. Milk the silly fool. But, as I've said, I can't get around like I used to. I'm by no means as well as I used to be. Old age isn't amusing.' Her eyes suddenly filled with tears. 'I don't want to lose him, Mr Samson. And that makes me as much of a fool as he.'

15

She reached into her handbag and took out a small lace-edged handkerchief. Samson waited until she had finished dabbing her eyes before saying, 'I couldn't commit myself to keeping an indefinite watch.'

'It won't be. A week away should be long enough.'

'Do you want divorce evidence?'

'Certainly not,' she replied sharply. 'I do not believe in divorce. No. I want to know where he goes and what he gets up to. I've cut down on his allowance but it doesn't seem to trouble him. I'm sure Robert has something to do with it. But Robert has been too fly by half for me. I'd like to get rid of him but I haven't a good reason and I know that if I did without reason he'd go to a tribunal and spill the beans. He's quite immoral.'

'Who is Robert?' Samson asked.

For the next few minutes he heard about a chauffeur-valet who had arrived on the scene two years previously with impeccable references. He was twenty-seven and claimed to be the son of a Scottish woman and a wealthy Egyptian. His father was dead and his mother lived in an apartment in Alexandria. She preferred sunshine and warmth to the cool highlands of her native land.

Robert had a pale olive skin, dark brown eyes and glossy black hair. He was, Mrs Huntingdon-Winstanley said, a born lady-killer. 'He can kill trollops with one flash from his eyes and, if so desired, can lay their panting bodies before his master.'

Her words, spoken with a rush of hyperbole, made her momentarily breathless. When she resumed speaking it was in a quieter voice. She said she was sure that Robert and Simon connived to deceive her.

'They are like a pair of boys, each encouraging the other in some juvenile game. I can remember the time I was in Simon's room and I found a black brassière, a wispy thing, wedged between the skirting-board and a chest of drawers. I summoned him at once and faced him

16

with the evidence. "Where did you get this?" I demanded to know. He became very shifty and began stuttering. Then Robert materialised from nowhere. Bold as brass he said, "So that's where it is. I must have dropped it when I was putting Mr Simon's shirts away." I said, "And what were you doing with a piece of women's underwear?" Do you know what he said?'

It wasn't a rhetorical question. She waited for Samson's answer. He made a guess. 'He said he was getting together an outfit for a fancy-dress party.'

'No. Nothing as obvious as that. Try again.'

Was she back to playing games? he wondered. The situation verged on unreality. Perhaps the old woman was indulging herself in some bizarre fantasy? Perhaps all she wanted was someone with whom to play games.

'Go on,' she said, 'how do you think Robert explained the brassière?'

All right, thought Samson, I'll play along. He said, 'I expect he was inventing a double-barrelled sling for sale to farmers as a dual-purpose piece of equipment. It could either hurl stones at crows raiding corn crops or be used as a support for cows with udder trouble.'

Mrs Huntingdon-Winstanley stiffened in her chair and sat very erect, a look of extreme displeasure on her face. If she had been a Roman empress Samson would have become instant fodder for hungry lions. 'If that is intended to be amusing,' she said icily, 'let me tell you I do not appreciate jokes about the females of any species. . . . No. Robert said that brassières of that particularly filmy texture were ideal for use as filters when draining a car's oil sump. I think he was having me on, but I couldn't argue. I don't know anything about cars. Do you know about cars?'

'I know something.'

'Does it make sense?'

Samson thought it sounded absurd but said, 'I've no idea.'

17

'Ha,' she barked.

Her habit of emitting a sharp 'Ha' puzzled him. It seemed to be a sound of multi-purpose use and its explosive delivery reminded him of a four-letter word he had often heard during an undistinguished career in the Royal Navy. That word had possessed a variety of meanings including, 'I've just dropped something on my foot', 'Is it my turn to go on watch already?' and 'I find the cancellation of shore leave most disappointing.'

'I thought people like you knew everything there was to know about cars,' she said. 'I hope you're the right man to catch out Robert and give me the evidence I need.'

Samson didn't care much for the assignment. It seemed a petty business. An old, invalid woman was trying to score off her husband's manservant and bring her husband to heel. Or rather, this was the case presented to him. It sometimes happened that the presented problem and the actual problem were very different.

'Well,' she said, 'are you the right man to get the evidence I want? You are what is called a private eye, are you not?'

Samson, who disliked this description, replied briskly, 'I can't answer that. I don't know. But if you have doubts, try someone else. You'll save money. I won't be sorry to over-price myself out of the market.'

'Ha! We are grumpy today, aren't we? . . . "I wouldn't be sorry to over-price myself out of the market,"' she mimicked in a voice as gruff as his. Then she laughed, the sort of laugh intended to deride whoever was the object of amusement.

He responded to her provocation with a bland smile. Her laughter died and a silence fell between them. The silence, compressed between the walls of a stuffy, unventilated room, was relieved only by the metronome tick of an elaborately over-decorated ormolu and white pillar clock which stood on a marble mantelpiece.

She broke the deadlock of silence, not with a word, but a wink. From a younger woman the wink might have been flirtatious but from her it was disturbingly out of character. Samson guessed she was trying to throw him off balance. He retained equilibrium by winking back. It was an odd grimace because he hadn't winked since he was a schoolboy. It made Mrs Huntingdon-Winstanley laugh.

'Oh, don't be silly,' she said. 'You mustn't take umbrage just because I ask if you're the right man for my problem.'

'I wish I knew what the problem was.'

'I've already told you.'

'I know what you've told me.'

'Oh, do stop being clever-clever,' she said disparagingly. 'You'll bore me if you go on like this.'

They were in verbal contest and Samson knew the time had come for him to take the initiative. Money doesn't talk but it reduces competition to basics, however crude. He came out of his corner with a financial punch. 'Let me make a thorough job of boring you,' he said. 'My fee for taking on this case will be five hundred pounds a day plus expenses. These can be heavy. I travel first-class and only drink and eat the best. If I want to get somewhere fast I think nothing of chartering a private aircraft and I would expect it to have a bar and a stewardess on board.'

'Good. I like men with expensive tastes. Thrifty men really do bore me.'

'I'm afraid you don't understand,' said Samson. 'I am known to be very thrifty. It is only with other people's money that I'm recklessly extravagant.'

'That's another thing I like about you. Honesty. Honest people are few and far between. I think we shall get along well, Mr Samson.'

He had the feeling that she'd won this round although in theory he was on to a very profitable deal. 'Tell me about your husband,' he said. 'How did you meet him?'

For the first time she looked uncertain. When she spoke

her voice was subdued. 'He was in a company founded by my grandfather. A junior salesman. In those days we made quality costume jewellery. Since then we've expanded into the popular market. Simon was given the south-west as his area. He did well and was awarded a bonus. That same day he requested a personal interview with me. I kept him waiting. Then – it must have been at least seven in the evening – I summoned him. He came in with a rose, a single red rose. He placed it on the table in front of me. "This", he said, "fulfils a promise I made myself if ever I should make the grade as one of your salesmen." And he turned on his heel and walked right out. I don't suppose you can imagine the effect it had on me. I was regarded by everyone as a dragon. Believe it or not, I was feared. And yet nobody suspected that the dragon had a romantic heart. But he did. He sensed it – the swine!' With the last two words her attitude changed and her voice resumed its hard authority.

'And after marriage?' enquired Samson.

'I'll not tell you that! Except, it went well for a while. But he's some years younger than me. We grew older and unhappier together. He had his peccadilloes but I was usually at hand to extricate him. And, if I wasn't, he'd come running back. Men who stray almost always run back to the familiar when things get too hot to handle. Simon was no different. He couldn't manage for long without me. And he was always so hopeless at covering up. He would stammer how sorry he was, that I was the only one he really cared for, and that would be the end of the matter. But since Robert, things have been different. I've got this horrible arthritis and I have days when I don't feel at all well.'

'And that's where I come in?'

'Yes. In spite of the impression I might have given, Simon isn't an uncultured man. He is not unlettered. Indeed, when he isn't being a fool he pursues his interests

20

in French literature. He is a Francophile.' She gestured towards the bookcase. 'Some of his book collection is over there. He makes as many visits to France as he can and scours the shops of antiquarian booksellers. At least, that's what he tells me he does. He always comes home with books and usually a gift for me, something exclusively French.'

'Like that clock?' asked Samson gazing at the mantelpiece. 'It's French, early nineteenth century, if I'm not mistaken. I've seen a similar one in Biggs of Maidenhead.'

'Well, well, you evidently are not altogether uncultivated. No, that clock belonged to my great-grandmother on my mother's side. I am descended from the Marquis de Maigny, you know. This was another reason why I was attracted to Simon. He was nothing but a salesman, Simon Smith by name, and yet he spoke fluent French and knew so much about France. I found it extraordinary and appealing.'

'Is he still Simon Smith?' Samson asked. 'Or are you Mrs Smith?'

'Heavens, no! I couldn't be Smith. I ask you! It was part of our agreement that he changed his name to mine. But that is by-the-way. Let me tell you my plan. He is due to pay another visit to France and will no doubt be accompanied by Robert. I want you to follow and see what they get up to. *What they get up to*, Mr Samson. Will you do that?'

Before replying Samson eased his bulk. The chair was hard and its seat not quite large enough to give full support. She noticed his discomfiture. 'You don't look very comfortable,' she said. 'Do you wish to sit elsewhere?'

He did, but if he moved too far the tape-recorder might be out of range of her voice. 'No, I'll stay put, thank you. And anyway, I'm not here to lounge about – '

'Ha!'

' – but to do business. I'd like to ask one or two

21

more questions before I commit myself to taking on your instructions.'

She leaned forward, elbows on table, chin cupped in hands. It was an attitude neither elegant nor aristocratic and Samson wondered if, in spite of material appearances to the contrary, he was dealing with some sort of pretentious phoney. This intuition struck swiftly and unexpectedly and as someone who had often relied on intuition he hung on to the fleeting impression. If she was a phoney, conning him, what possible motive could she have? He would want to see the colour of her money before moving an inch on the case.

'Go ahead,' she said. 'What do you want to know?'

'Before anything else, I shall require a handsome payment in advance before I take any action.'

'I understand,' she said, and there was a note of impatience in her voice. 'We are not, I trust, going to engage in argument about money. This is an English lady's drawing room, not an Arab merchant's bazaar.'

'Quite. But I must refer to your financial arrangements with your husband.'

She took her elbows from the table and sat back, stiffly upright. 'If you must,' she said wearily.

Undeterred by her evident distaste of the subject Samson said, 'You gave him an allowance which, apparently, you have reduced. If you stopped the allowance altogether it would, to coin a phrase, clip his wings.'

'It might, but I certainly wouldn't reduce it any more. As a matter of fact, if it's so important to you, the reduction is fairly nominal. A token of my disesteem. No, money is a lever I will not use against him. I won't have the memory of a rose spoiled. He can *know* I have the power. It can be something to worry him. But I would never dream of using it. I still have the rose, faded, shrivelled, withered. It is, among other things, a symbol that money didn't come between us. I would never try to keep him by using my power over his finances. I probably sound like a silly, sentimental old woman, and maybe I am. . . . What other questions do you have? I hope they won't be too tedious.'

'I'd like to know how long you've been married.'

'A great number of years, Mr Samson.'

He nodded. 'I thought so. But how many exactly?'

'Oh, twenty-nine.' She spoke as though she was making a random selection for a wager in a game of roulette.

Samson, head bowed over notepad, wrote, 'm. 29'. Without lifting his head he said, 'Could I have your first name, please?'

'Really! I don't see how that can be relevant, but if you must know, it's Sybil.'

After writing down the name he looked up at her. 'I should like to have a photo of your husband,' he said.

'I'll give you one before you leave.'

'And do you have a photo of Robert?'

The question seemed to astonish Mrs Huntingdon-Winstanley. 'What an extraordinary thing to ask,' she said. 'Of course I don't have a photograph of Robert. Except for nannies who are of a rather different class, one never has photographs of servants.'

It was Samson's turn to seem surprised. 'Why not?' he asked.

'Well, one just doesn't. That's all there is to it.'

'I see. . . . Speaking of Robert, if his father was a wealthy Egyptian, why is he nothing more than a chauffeur-valet?'

'Ha! Well might you ask. His story is that his mother in Alexandria has all the money and he, Robert, has quarrelled with her. They aren't even on speaking terms. Believe that, if you will. I don't.'

Samson gave a smile, revealing perfectly even, small white teeth set in an expanse of pink gum. 'That sounds like healthy scepticism,' he said. 'What is Robert's surname?'

'Mansour.'

23

As he wrote Samson spelled the name aloud. 'Have I got it right?' he asked.

'Quite right. I believe it's a common name in Egypt.'

'Just what one would expect,' said Samson with a hint of mockery in his voice.

'Exactly.'

'When your husband goes to France does he travel by air?'

'No. He takes the car over by ferry. You can follow him in your car.'

'That could be a problem, but we'll leave it aside for the moment. Could you tell me a little more about your company's business?'

'I don't see what that has to do with the matter in hand.'

'I'd like to know.'

'Very well. We are a private company although we may go public. We supply some of the major chain stores with costume jewellery. We must know in advance what the fashion dress of the season will be so that the jewellery can match or contrast. For example, the sweater suit requires fairly big chunky jewellery to provide contrast with the suit. We've gone down market in the last few years and use plastic, wood and glass, and we manufacture co-ordinating belts, brooches, bangles and hair accessories as well as straightforward costume jewellery, or junk jewellery, as they call it nowadays. Our latest designs are geometric.'

She spoke with the confidence of full authority and Samson was prompted to ask, 'Are you still active in the business?'

'Not as a director,' she replied, 'but I am a majority shareholder.'

'What is the company's name?'

'Gemtrix.'

'Does your husband have an interest in the company?'

'Not any more. He left after our marriage with a golden

handshake. He got through that, of course. He depends on an allowance now, and don't ask what it is because I shan't tell you.'

After making a few notes Samson looked across the table and asked, 'When is his next visit to France?'

'In three days. I can't at the moment give you the exact time he's booked for the ferry but I'll call you tonight about that.'

Samson nodded. 'Fine, provided you understand my terms for this assignment. These—'

She interrupted him, overriding his voice with, 'I don't care about your terms. Charge what you will, I'll pay.'

'I shall need a thousand-pound advance.'

'You shall have it,' she replied instantly. 'I hate talking about money. It's so vulgar, and I'd be obliged if you would refrain from mentioning it again. You will be paid, and paid well. That's the end of it. What else do you want to know?' Before he could answer she went on, 'I hope you haven't got one of those horrid answerphones. If you have, I shan't use it.'

With every difficulty she raised Samson mentally increased his fee. 'If you 'phone my office during the evening you will be confronted with precisely that piece of useful technological innovation,' he said.

'In that case I'd like your private number.'

She didn't so much look at him, or stare; she glared. He was reminded of a teacher at his school who, because he had stumbled over a definition in a physics lesson, had made him write out a hundred times, 'The moment of a force about an axis is the product of that force and the perpendicular distance between the axis and the line of action of the force.' It had been incomprehensible then, and it had remained incomprehensible.

But he wasn't a schoolboy any more, and he was no longer intimidated by authoritarian demands. 'If I give you my private number,' he said, 'any call you make will cost, at the very least, an extra hundred pounds on top of my normal charge.'

She bunched her fist and hit the table with such a moment of force that the axis of the pile of spillikins was shattered and the little pieces of ivory were scattered over the table-top. 'I will not discuss money! Charge what you like!'

Samson ripped a sheet from his notepad and wrote a number. 'I've recently moved my home address,' he said, 'and I'm expecting to move my business premises too. This is my new private number.'

He folded the paper and handed it to her across the table.

She opened the paper and read out the number. 'Numerology interests me,' she said. 'This number adds up to nine, my lucky number. That's good.' She reached down and put the paper into her handbag. And then she gave a smile which was unexpectedly gentle, even shy. 'I'd like to give you a little souvenir of our meeting,' she said. 'How about one of my spillikins? Are you attracted by any particular one?'

Samson was; he had noticed it almost immediately. It was a tiny replica of a longcase clock, exquisitely carved. But her change of demeanour from masked aggression, when they had seemed to be in combat, to the vulnerable look of a young girl in an old woman's body made Samson feel off balance. What she hadn't achieved by mockery, snobbery, or the surprising wink, she had attained by lowering her defences. He realised it was important to her that he selected something. 'I should greatly value that little clock,' he said.

'It's yours. I'm so glad. It is delightful, isn't it?' She reached for her stick and rose awkwardly to her feet and then hobbled across the room to a bell-push. 'I'll ask Jennifer to help me upstairs and I'll get you the photo. Wait here, if you will. I shan't be long.'

She was out of the room for about five minutes and

Samson, more from professional habit of sweeping a room for electronic bugs than from suspicion, wandered around checking fittings customarily used for such devices. He didn't expect to find anything, and he didn't in his short tour of the room.

When she returned to the room he noticed that one foot seemed to be dragging as she hobbled towards the table. 'There you are,' she said, 'a photograph of my husband and a cheque for one thousand pounds.'

Samson put both items in his briefcase. 'Thank you for the little clock,' he said. 'I'll be on my way now.'

His right hand moved up slightly, ready to accept the handshake he thought she might offer. She noticed the slight movement and recoiled, and he knew he was regarded not as a professional man but as a servant. Ladies did not shake hands with servants.

He gave a faint smile and bowed deeply. 'Good day, Mrs Huntingdon-Winstanley.'

'Good day, Mr Samson. . . . Oh, and there is one other thing I feel it's fair to tell you.'

Samson raised his eyebrows. 'Yes?'

'You aren't the first detective I've employed. I had another man about two months ago. He was following my husband and Robert to the south coast but most unfortunately had an accident.'

Samson's eyebrows remained lifted. 'Was he badly hurt?'

'He was killed.'

'What sort of accident?' Samson enquired.

'Oh, it's no use asking me. As I've told you, I know absolutely nothing about cars. I believe the brakes on his car failed completely while he was going fast round a corner.'

'Was any other driver involved?'

'I don't think so. I only mention it because I think you should be careful.' Her eyes, two sapphires set in a thick cosmetic mask, looked at him with a peculiar penetration. 'Very careful,' she added.

27

'I take your point,' said Samson. 'What was the name of this man?'

'Brightwell.'

Samson thought. 'That's a name which means nothing to me.'

'Possibly not. But who you don't know is no concern of mine.' She turned to the maid who was standing in a dutifully deferential attitude by the door. 'Jennifer will see you out. Good day again.'

Chapter 2

Shandy looked up from her word-processor as he walked into their office, flicked a strand of long blonde hair off her forehead, and said, 'I've had nine callers on the phone about your clocks.'

Samson was in the process of selling his collection of antique clocks but he didn't want to talk about the dispersal of a collection which had taken more than half his lifetime to acquire; instead, he said, 'What a coincidence. Nine is Mrs Huntingdon-Winstanley's lucky number.'

Shandy, who had the cool beauty of a Scandinavian starlet, and was Samson's professional alter ego and, when it came to dietary matters, his alter super-ego, frowned and said, 'She isn't into black magic, is she?'

He went to a small annexe where there was a sink, an electric ring and a small refrigerator. He took out a can of lager from the fridge, reached for a schooner glass on a shelf, and answered Shandy's question with, 'Why do you ask?'

'Nine is a mystical number, isn't it? Three times three is the perfect numerical plural. A trinity of trinities. The weird sisters in *Macbeth* sang its praises when they wanted "the charm wound up".'

Samson shook his head. 'I sometimes think it was a mistake for you to take that Open University degree. No, she isn't into black magic – not so far as I know. She's an old woman who wants me to keep tabs on her husband.'

'How old?'

He tipped the lager into the glass. 'Funny you should ask that. I want you to pop down to St Catherine's House. She was married to a Simon Smith about twenty-nine years ago. Her age will appear in the records.'

'You could have asked her.'

'If I had I should have got a frosty answer: "Mr Samson, one does not ask a lady her age."'

Shandy laughed. 'She was like that, was she? Sort of well-bred?'

'Sort of. Or a very good imitation.' He took a drink. 'That's better. When you transcribe the tape you'll understand why I kept personal questions to a minimum.'

He went on to tell her about the interview and concluded by saying, 'On my way back here I made a decision.'

Anyone but Shandy, who knew him well, would have expected the decision to relate to what he had just been saying. She knew it would be something totally unconnected and, anticipating a change of direction, she clapped her hands in delight and said, 'You've decided to give me a rise.'

'That's right,' he said. 'That's what I've decided.'

If he had told her that porcupines were taking over the world she couldn't have looked more startled. 'You are?'

'Yes.'

'I was only joking. You're not joking too?'

'No. This is a period of change. I've got a new flat and now I want to move the business up-market to the West End. Since it's going to be all change, and I don't want to lose you, I thought it was the right time for a rise.'

'There's never a wrong time for a rise.' She stood up and looked out of the window. 'It's started raining. The forecast was for intermittent showers. I'll need this.' She went to the door and took a pink raincoat off a hook.

'Where are you going?'

'St Catherine's House. What's her first name?'

'Sybil.'

'At least you had the nerve to ask that. What about her husband? Do you want me to check him out?'

Samson thought. 'Yes. She said he was sixty-five and Simon Smith until he changed his surname to hers after marriage. You could check that out but don't spend too much time on it.' She buttoned up her raincoat. 'See you,' she said.

It was late that afternoon, and after she had returned to the office, that Shandy buzzed Samson's intercom and told him that a Mr Winstanley had arrived without an appointment. 'Can you see him?' she asked.

Her visit to St Catherine's House had proved fruitless. She had been unable to find any record of Mrs Huntingdon-Winstanley's marriage.

'I'll see him,' said Samson. 'Show him in.'

Winstanley had silver, wavy hair and a florid complexion, and his eyes were of almost the same bright blue as his wife's. He was wearing a well-cut charcoal grey lounge suit with a carnation in the buttonhole and red silk kerchief poking like an insolent tongue from the breast pocket. He was a man who looked in very good shape for his age.

Without invitation he took a chair and placed it in front of Samson's desk. 'I won't waste your time or mine,' he said as he sat down. 'I'm here to tell you to drop the assignment my wife gave you. She's a sick woman and not responsible for what she does. Highly embarrassing, but there you are. I'll recompense you for wasted time. Will a hundred pounds settle the matter?'

Samson leaned back in his swivel chair and placed the fingertips of each hand together so that they formed an arch over his ample stomach. With an expression of benign indulgence on his face he might have been a kindly priest being visited by a parishioner.

31

'I'm surprised your wife told you about our little chat,' he said.

Winstanley ignored the comment. 'The poor dear suffers from delusions and then comes to her senses,' he said.

'And what was the delusion in this instance?' Samson asked smoothly.

Winstanley began drumming his fingers on the arm of the chair and Samson noticed the glitter of a diamond ring on the little finger. He couldn't tell whether it was a fake but it was certainly not the sort of ring usually worn by men.

'This is most distasteful,' said Winstanley. 'I much dislike discussing private matters with someone of your calling – if it can be termed a calling – but my wife suffers periodically from the delusion that I'm unfaithful to her. It's absolute rubbish, of course. But there you are. She's obsessed with the notion.' The fingers stopped drumming and he pointed at Samson. 'You aren't the first fellow in your trade to be hired by her, you know.'

'Is that so? And what did the other fellow discover?'

'Nothing. Absolutely nothing, of course.'

Samson reached out to a silver cigar-box and selected a panatella.

'Would you like one?' he asked.

'Thank you, no.'

'You mentioned my trade. What do you regard as my trade, Mr Winstanley?'

'I believe you call yourself a private detective. I'd call you an invader of privacy.'

Samson shook his head. 'I'm a private investigator and security adviser,' he said. 'I'll give you my card if you like.'

Winstanley grimaced as if he'd been offered an oily rag. 'No, thank you.'

Samson struck a match and looked over the flame at the man who had come to see him. 'And what is *your* trade?' he asked, and then, apparently inattentive to any reply, concentrated on lighting his cigar.

'That's none of your business,' said Winstanley.

Samson dropped the spent match in an ashtray. 'It is my business while your wife is my client.'

If looks could have killed Samson and his cigar would have both been reduced to instant ash and anyone within a range of ten miles would have been seared by the flash of anger in Winstanley's eyes. 'I'm not going to bandy words with you, Samson. Will a hundred and fifty pounds meet your bill?'

Samson regarded the fringe of untroubled ash on his cigar. After considering it for a few moments he said, 'You called me an invader of privacy, but what are you doing? You are invading my privacy. I didn't ask you to come here and I'm not a public service.'

For a moment it looked as if Winstanley might explode but with an obvious effort at self-control he modified his voice. 'Look here, let's be sensible about this, old man. Let's not waste each other's time. How much?'

Samson smiled. Whenever someone of Winstanley's generation and class addressed him as 'old man' or 'old chap' it meant that the sting had gone out of their demands. He said, 'Waste time? I can waste food, I can waste money, I can waste my life, but Time I cannot waste. Time is immutable, not mine to waste, spend or dispose of.'

Winstanley's jawline hardened. 'How much?'

'My services aren't for sale to you. Until your wife cancels her instructions, she is my client.'

Although he maintained a rigid self-control every syllable of what Winstanley said was edged with frustration. He made a last attempt at conciliation. 'To be frank, and your attitude forces me to say this, my wife is quite irresponsible. I'm seriously thinking of a separation even though I realise she'd go to pieces if I left her. Your interference in our

33

domestic life can only aggravate the situation. Do I make myself plain?'

'What you've said is plain, but I've still got a job to do. I'm not a marriage guidance counsellor, but that's what you and your wife seem to need.'

'So you're going ahead?'

'I shall follow my instructions.'

'And what are your instructions?'

'That is confidential.'

Winstanley stood up. 'Then don't be surprised if unpleasant consequences follow.'

'Is that a threat?'

'Take it how you like.'

'"Surprised by unpleasant consequences",' Samson mused. 'I wonder what makes you think unpleasant consequences should surprise me. In my occupation it is the pleasant consequences which surprise.'

Winstanley stood up. 'I've had enough of this. Good day.'

He marched out of the room, head held high.

The moment the door had closed behind him Samson rose from his seat. As he passed Shandy he motioned her to be silent. For a big man he could move with stealth and he followed Winstanley into the street. Waiting on a double yellow line was a parked Jaguar XJ-S Coupé. A young olive-skinned man, whom Samson presumed was Robert, opened the passenger door for Winstanley. Samson memorised the car's number-plate and then went into a nearby shop.

Chapter 3

Shandy walked into Samson's room and suddenly stopped. 'They've gone,' she said, gazing at a blank wall which had faintly discoloured marks where a row of antique clocks had once hung.

'I've decided to put them up for auction, after all,' he said. 'They were collected last night.'

'It makes the place look quite bare.'

'Do you mind?'

She shook her head and the wayward strand of blonde hair fell across her forehead. She brushed it back. At one time this mannerism had irritated Samson but with familiarity he had grown to like it. He was old enough to be her parent and during the years they had worked together had become something of a father-figure to her. Theirs had developed into an intimate but asexual relationship in which he tolerated her attempts to make him diet and occasionally to boss or tease him, and she came to him for advice on almost everything except the upbringing of her daughter.

'This afternoon,' he said, 'I'm going to view a vacant premises in the St James area. It would be very convenient. Only a stone's throw from my flat.' He reached out for a paper on the side of his desk. 'Would you fax this to Curtis, Soames and Co? It's the report they wanted in a hurry.'

She took the paper. 'Has Mrs H-W been in touch yet?'

'No.'

'Thought she was going to call you last night.'

'Presumably she isn't yet sure of the exact time her old man is going abroad.' He stood up. 'You're right. The place does look bare. If we were staying on I'd have it redecorated.' And then, changing the subject, but not the tone of his voice, 'I'm going out. Don't know when I'll be back.'

'Where are you going?'

'There's an underground garage at Mrs H-W's apartment block. I'm going to see if I can strike lucky and find a Jaguar XJ-S Coupé.'

'Take care,' she said, and her voice was serious. 'I've got a feeling this case could get quite nasty.'

'My feeling too,' he said.

Before entering the building Samson spent a few minutes studying the exterior. He then went in through pressure-operated doors and walked across a polished parquet-floored hall to where a uniformed security guard sat at a desk on which a telephone and two television monitors were mounted.

The guard looked up. 'Morning, sir.'

'Good morning. I was here yesterday.'

'Yes, I remember.'

'Has my umbrella been handed in by Mrs Huntingdon-Winstanley or one of her staff?'

'Not to me it hasn't.'

Samson allowed disappointment to cloud his face. 'I thought I must have left it here, but maybe I'm wrong.'

The guard reached for the telephone. 'I'll give them a buzz if you like, sir.'

'No, I'd rather you didn't.' Samson lowered his voice. 'I might be hired to do a job of work for the Winstanleys and I don't want to give the wrong impression. Don't want to bother them. They don't seem the easiest of employers.'

The guard's lips twitched in a stillborn smile. 'You can say that again.'

'I'll forget about the brolly. I could have left it in the pub I went to afterwards.' Still with lowered voice Samson said, 'I don't suppose you've got a loo here. I don't like troubling you but I've got a bladder condition. I'm taking tablets but they haven't started working yet.'

The guard looked around furtively as though afraid of being overheard. 'These are all private apartments. Very private, if you take my meaning . . . I'm not supposed to . . . But I don't suppose it would harm. I know what it must be like. My Dad had a dodgy bladder too. Look, there's a toilet at the back, strictly for staff only.'

While he was speaking Samson had produced a five pound note which he folded and discreetly pushed under one of the monitors. 'That's very kind of you,' he said. 'How do I get to it?'

The guard pointed towards a corridor. 'You see them rubber tree plants. Down there. Past them.'

'Very kind,' Samson repeated. 'Excuse me for asking, but what staff use it?'

'Well, there's me and my lot, and chauffeurs who don't live in, and the like.'

The information was exactly what Samson needed. If the convenience was provided for chauffeurs, among others, it was almost certainly within easy access of the underground garage. The only problem now would be to neutralise the television monitors which showed pictures of the garage's interior.

'Very kind,' he repeated yet again as he moved away. He walked past tall rubber plants, the dark green leathery leaves of which were dulled by dust, and reached a door which was embellished with the tiny outline of a trousered male figure. Samson walked on past the door and came almost at once to a wide staircase beside a service elevator.

37

Without pausing he descended the stairs and found himself at the internal entrance to the garage. It was lighted by neon strips. He looked around for the closed-circuit TV cameras and spotted one high on a wall in one corner. A second camera was mounted on the adjacent corner so that the whole area could be kept under surveillance. Both had zoom lenses worked electrically by small motors.

Under each camera there was a blind spot and Samson knew that if he could reach these spots undetected he could immobilise the cameras either by masking the lens, interfering with the printed circuit boards within the sides of the cameras or by disconnecting the cables supplying the electric current.

Outwardly he made no sound but inwardly he sighed deeply. He hated it when, in the course of duty, he was required to crawl on hands and knees, but this demeaning action was now necessary if he was to take advantage of the shadows cast by car wheels.

Not for the first time in his career he found his knowledge of security devices invaluable. Within a minute he had disabled both cameras. During his crawl he had seen the sleek two-door Jaguar and he now hurried towards it, fishing in his pocket for skeleton car keys. It was a matter of moments before the lid of the boot was opened and a miniaturised radio transmitter put in place.

He would now be able to follow the car at a distance, well out of sight of its occupants. As he closed and locked the car boot he felt well satisfied with this piece of investigative pre-planning. But his moment of triumph was short-lived. Just as he was about to return to the cameras to reconnect leads he heard voices.

Mentally he used the four-letter word he had heard so frequently during service with the Royal Navy. The guard would by now have seen that the monitor screens were blank and might be on his way to investigate. On the other hand, and this was what Samson had counted on, he might be telephoning his headquarters to report that the closed-circuit television had broken down and asking for an engineer to be sent to repair the fault.

Cautiously he lifted his head to view the internal garage entrance. The voices were clearer and belonged to a couple of men. As they came into view he saw Robert with a fair-haired young man. He ducked his head. The voices were now quite clear.

Robert said, 'See you soon.' and the other man replied, 'You bet.'

There was the sound of a car engine starting and then daylight flooded into the garage as electronically operated gates opened. A car drove away and the gates closed.

Samson waited for Robert to leave. Seconds were ticking past and, with every second, he was in greater danger of discovery.

Against his expectations, the sound of Robert's footsteps on the garage's concrete surface instead of diminishing became louder. Samson realised he was approaching the Jaguar and, unless evasive action was taken, discovery was inevitable.

He crept round the car's blind side. Everything would now depend on whether Robert was making for the front or the back of the Jaguar.

Samson, crouching by the front, was unlucky. The footsteps were directed towards the front. He flexed his muscles.

As Robert rounded the car's bonnet two-hundred-and-thirty-eight pounds of battering ram were launched at his midriff. He gasped as a hard head impacted against his stomach, reeled back and, before he could recover or see his assailant, had been knocked unconscious with a well-directed punch to the jaw.

With a swiftness which would have amazed people who thought him lazy, Samson raced to the cameras, rapidly reconnected cables, and sped up the staircase.

As he reached the rubber plants he slowed his pace and strolled towards the desk where the guard was trying to adjust the knobs on one of the monitors. 'Having trouble?' he asked.

'I was. These both went off. One has come back, and the other is still on the blink.'

In his hurry the connection of one camera had been faulty. But this consideration didn't trouble Samson. He was more concerned with making a casual exit. He said, 'I don't know who's in charge of the maintenance work here but the rubber plants need sponging. There's a disgraceful amount of dust on the leaves. I'd report it to management if I were you.'

'Right, sir. I will.'

Having given helpful advice Samson strolled out of the building.

Back at his office Shandy asked, 'How did it go?'

Samson told her.

'Do you think Robert will report it?' she asked.

'If he does, and the guard admits to having allowed me to use the staff loo, it's obvious where suspicion will fall. But if the guard decides to keep mum, and he might, then I'm all right. After all, he shouldn't have allowed an outsider to go into private quarters.'

'But you might be suspected anyway.'

'Possibly, but I'm already in the enemy camp. What matters is that the bug I've planted isn't found.'

'What if it is?'

'Then I shan't be able to follow when they land in France.'

Shandy looked perturbed. 'I don't think they'll let it rest at that. I didn't like the look of that toy pensioner who was in here yesterday. I think he'll have it in for you whether the bug is found or not.'

'Woman's intuition?' he asked.

She narrowed her eyes. 'That sounds remarkably like male arrogance.'

He grinned. 'I didn't mean it like that. I respect intuitions. I even have them myself sometimes. In the trade they're known as hunches. But I can't let myself be ruled by them. What is an intuition, anyway, but a perception not gained through intelligence or reason. I am, as you know, eminently intelligent and reasonable and must back these qualities against someone else's intuition.'

She groaned. 'If I have to listen to a talking dictionary I certainly deserve that rise you've promised and not yet delivered.'

'You'll get it,' said Samson. 'I'm a man of my word.'

'Too many words sometimes,' she replied and continued the typing his entrance had interrupted.

Samson's new flat was on the third floor of a late nineteenth-century building in an area of London's West End where small art galleries and shops selling antique silver display wares without ostentation or price tags. It was a district which contrasted with the part of south London where he had previously lived and still had an office, a district where unoccupied premises were daubed with graffiti, and there were always some shops having closing-down sales with posters screaming 'slashed prices'. Not that small shops didn't exist in his new environment where such humble needs as the purchase of a hammer and nails, takeaway coffee, or shoe repairs could be met, but these services were tidily out of sight in a narrow alleyway, Crown Passage, which linked King Street to Pall Mall.

Before taking on a fourteen-year lease Samson had reconnoitred the area and decided he could be as content here as anywhere in the capital city. Parks and good restaurants were close by and although he had no interest in clubs it was an advantage to live in the centre of clubland because it was plentifully supplied with taxis. Samson didn't care much for walking along crowded pavements not only because he had a predisposition towards indolence but his bulk made accidental collisions with pedestrians a high percentage likelihood.

After many years of regarding an apartment simply as a place to eat and sleep in, he experienced pleasurable surprise at his own reactions on taking over a well-furnished and maintained luxury flat. That it was a ready-made home reflecting someone else's taste didn't trouble him; he liked the decor and comfort.

During the day the street below his flat was clotted with cars and, on busy sidewalks, the pedestrians were a cosmopolitan mix – office workers of different nationalities, well-wined men with well-lined bank accounts weaving their ways to clubs which were refuges from the despised social and sexual egalitarianism of late twentieth-century Britain, art dealers scurrying along with canvas under each arm, tourists posing beside a chunk of metal which looked like an elephant's rump but was an abstract sculpture designed to enhance the piazza by the high-rise Economist building, robed Arabs and Africans on their way to conference rooms, and students with holdalls carrying books borrowed from the London Library.

Samson, who was in a sense a professional observer, and sometimes paid voyeur, enjoyed watching, whether it was shipping in a busy waterway, or passing life viewed from a cafe's pavement table. He was glad to have found a home on the third floor of a building from where variable elements of humanity could be seen moving against a backdrop of stone, brick and concrete.

At night there was less activity and this was something he knew he'd miss. At his previous place late-working Asians kept their shops open until nearly midnight and the strains of reggae and rap were never far away. On the evening of the day when he'd planted a bug in the Jaguar's boot he decided to take a stroll. Soho was less than a mile away and here he could find a good restaurant and some of the noise and colour which he was missing. It would also give him an opportunity to explore the territory and discover new precincts and passageways.

Ignoring Shandy's carefully planned calorie-controlled diet sheet he enjoyed a meal at a German restaurant in Greek Street before making his way back to his flat. It was while walking down a dimly lit alleyway which provided a short cut that a sixth sense made him swerve and duck as a blow aimed from behind grazed his shoulder. He swung round and grabbed his attacker's coat. The other man dropped a length of lead piping and wrenched himself free. In the shadowy half-light a gleam of metal suddenly appeared in his hand. As he lunged, Samson side-stepped and brought his own hand down in a slicing cut on the other's wrist. A knife clattered to the ground as the attacker yelped with pain. A moment later he was scampering away.

Samson respected his digestive processes too much to attempt pursuit. Instead, he stooped and picked up the abandoned knife. It was an ordinary flick-knife of a make he recognised. After retracting the blade he slipped it into his pocket and continued on his way.

In the course of his career he had made a few enemies and fewer friends. His assailant looked white, with close-cropped hair, sunken eyes and pock-marked cheeks. He had been about the same height as Samson but only half as broad. He might have been a common mugger or a paid hit-man acting on behalf of someone who had sworn to get revenge some day.

Samson proceeded on his way without hurry. He'd had enough exercise for one night and regretted his decision not to take a taxi from the restaurant. If this was a sample of what went on after nightfall he'd have to be as watchful as he'd been in the environs of south London.

As he turned the key to the front door of his flat

he heard the telephone ringing. Without undue haste he discarded his raincoat before picking up a handset in the small entrance hall.

'Samson here.'

'Oh, Mr Samson, I've been trying to get you.'

He recognised the caller's voice instantly.

'You've got some information for me, Mrs Huntingdon-Winstanley?'

'I have indeed. I must be quick. Was it you who assaulted Robert in the garage?'

'I've no idea what you're talking about,' lied Samson.

'They think it must have been. There has been a commotion. Someone unauthorised got into the underground garage and when Robert went down there he was ambushed and beaten up in a most cowardly way. I gather that he didn't have a chance to defend himself. There's been an enquiry and the doorman's been dismissed. But that's not the point. I know how my husband's mind works, particularly when he's encouraged by Robert. Be on your guard against being harmed, Mr Samson.'

Samson smiled to himself. Her warning was late but appreciated. 'How thoughtful of you to call,' he said. 'As a matter of interest, why do Mr Winstanley and Robert think I'm involved in this fracas?'

'Before he was dismissed the doorman admitted to having allowed you to use the staff lavatory. He said you'd come in search of an umbrella but you had been – as the vulgar saying has it – taken short. Is that correct?'

'I'd prefer not to comment on such a personal matter as I'm sure a lady of your distinction would understand,' replied Samson smoothly, 'but I will say this. I would strenuously deny any allegations of assault. In any event, isn't the garage monitored by cameras? The attack must have been videoed.'

'That's not so. Apparently the television was out of order for a few minutes, probably sabotaged.'

'Quite extraordinary,' Samson murmured. 'I wonder who could have done such a thing.'

A faint chuckle came down the line. 'To be honest, I must say I got a sort of naughty pleasure out of Robert's misfortune. A little harmless *schadenfreude*. Incidentally, Robert spent all afternoon making sure the car hadn't been tampered with.'

'Did he find anything?'

'I've no idea. But he took it out for a run and it seemed all right. Now then, listen carefully. They've changed their plans. They've booked a passage for tomorrow. The four o'clock sailing from Dover to Boulogne. I know this is very short notice but can you manage it? And please don't bore me with talk of how much extra this change of plan will cost.'

'I don't have my diary with me,' said Samson, 'and I'm not sure of tomorrow's engagements. Can I call you in the morning?'

'No, you'd better not. My husband has been highly offensive to me on account of your visit and what we discussed. It seems that everything was overheard. I'm inclined to suspect that Jennifer might be a fifth columnist, but I can't be sure.' Her voice became strained and Samson detected a note of fear. 'He looked at me with murder in his eyes. If he should intercept a call from you, I don't know what he'd do.'

'In that case,' said Samson, 'I'll make sure you get a call after they've left on the car ferry. It will either be from me to say I couldn't make it or from my secretary to say I could.'

'Thank you.'

'By the way, did your husband tell you he'd been to see me? He wanted me to drop the assignment.'

'Did he? Oh, you won't, will you? You'll stick by me, won't you?'

The old adage, 'He who pays the piper calls the tune'

floated into Samson's mind but he simply said, 'Yes, I'll stick by you.'

'And, Mr Samson, if anything should happen to me . . . Anything untoward, I mean . . . If I should die in suspicious circumstances . . .'

'I'll investigate. Rest assured.'

'Thank you so much. And now I must go. Good night.'

Chapter 4

Samson was at his office early the following morning. He decided certain appointments could be postponed and Shandy could deal with the others. When she arrived sixteen seconds after her usual starting time of nine o'clock he looked ostentatiously at his watch and said, 'Late again.'

'What are you doing here? Couldn't you sleep?'

He told her of the previous evening's events.

'Do you think it was an ordinary mugging attempt,' she asked, 'or was the guy working for Winstanley?'

'I'm keeping an open mind with a bias towards mugging. I think Winstanley would try something more sophisticated and, anyway, I don't think I was being tailed to and from the restaurant. But we'll leave that aside for the present. I've decided to take a trip to France and you're going to earn your rise. I want— '

'Just a minute,' she interrupted, 'we haven't discussed yet what my rise is to be.'

'Don't bore me with talk of money,' said Samson in a fair attempt at mimicry of Mrs Huntingdon-Winstanley. 'I want you to book me on a car ferry. Air ferry. Southend to le Touquet. It's essential that I arrive at le Touquet by three in the afternoon to give me enough time to drive to Boulogne to meet the sea ferry which leaves Dover at four. If you can't book me on a public service, ring around and get a private contractor. No expense spared.'

'You don't want to be bored with talk of money?'

'That's right.'

She shook her head. 'I never thought I'd hear you say that.'

With his specially equipped Ford Granada Samson was ferried by air to le Touquet. From the airport he drove north to the car ferry terminal at Boulogne. He arrived twenty minutes before the ferry was due and waited in a parking space just outside the dock exit. The sky above was overcast with pale grey cloud and seagulls wheeled and cried above grey dock buildings. It was a bleak scene.

Samson was aware that if the planted transmitter had been discovered and destroyed he wouldn't be able to follow his quarry without high risk of being detected. The equipment housed in his car was the latest refinement of advanced surveillance technology. Radio signals emitted by the transmitter (if it was still in place) would be picked up by an aerial on the Granada and passed to a receiver tuned to the same frequency as the transmitter. In the receiver the signals would be converted to appear on a small screen, mounted on the car's dashboard, as a series of blips moving from left to right. The closer the blips were to each other the closer he would be to the car he was following. A calibration at the bottom of the screen gave a guide to the distance between the blips in kilometres and fractions of kilometres but there was also a small digital display panel which gave a fairly exact measurement of the distance between transmitter and receiver. The reliable range of the transmitter was up to ten kilometres provided there were no abnormal environmental factors.

As he waited, Samson ate one of his pre-packed sandwiches supplied by Shandy who had also provided a thermos flask of coffee. The sandwiches were filled with a low-calorie spread and the coffee was unsweetened. She was, he reflected, carrying her diet campaign to unacceptable extremes. Next time he would buy his own takeaway snacks.

He put the refreshments away when cars from the ferry emerged from the exit. The eleventh to appear was the Jaguar with Robert at the wheel and Winstanley seated beside him. They passed without a glance in the direction of the parked Granada. Samson started the car's engine and turned to follow. This was the crucial moment when he'd find out whether the transmitter had been discovered.

He reached forward and switched on the receiver mounted on the dashboard and almost at once green blips began passing across the screen. His venture into the underground garage and the journey to Boulogne wouldn't be wasted.

He trailed the Jaguar at a respectful distance until it reached the town's outskirts and took the road south into open country. Long stretches of featureless agricultural land between villages made the countryside seem still locked in the grip of winter. Only here and there flecks of green on bare-branched trees showed that a new season was striving to break the shackles of the old. Above, the sky had become a grey shroud which was slowly darkening as it was drawn over the dying day.

The Jaguar travelled fast on the fairly straight and open road and within two hours it was approaching Rouen. By this time all cars were using headlights and Samson closed in to a distance of three hundred metres confident that the chance of being detected as a follower was negligible. But his confidence made him too casual. Suddenly he was aware that the blips on the screen were travelling fast and almost linked in an unbroken line. He braked as he passed a sign showing he was entering the village of Quincampoix. Pulling into the kerb he came to a stop.

Ahead he could see Robert getting out of the car and walking to the back. For a moment he wondered if the boot was to be opened but then Winstanley also got out of the car and it was evident they were changing positions and Winstanley was now going to drive. Perhaps he'd become bored with being a passenger or maybe he could find his way through Rouen which Samson knew, from past experience, was no easier than getting through London in the rush-hour.

The pause gave him a chance to glance at a road map. It seemed possible that once the cars were past Rouen the Jaguar would continue east towards Paris. However, once clear of Rouen, and on the A13 to Paris, Samson was surprised when after a few kilometres the Jaguar left the autoroute and continued south after stopping at a toll booth. No longer too casual he kept his distance and handed over his payment when the Jaguar was out of sight.

Having ruled out Paris as a destination Samson wondered where the trip would end. The possibilities were almost inexhaustible. He hoped it wouldn't be as far as Bordeaux or, even more distant, Biarritz.

The Jaguar by-passed Évreux and Samson ate the last of his unappetising sandwiches. He was beginning to wish he hadn't taken on the assignment when it was clear from the screen and speedometer that the Jaguar was slowing down and then the blips became more spaced out and fainter. He pulled into the side of the road. Somehow he had lost the other car. It must have turned off the main road. Taking his car into a tight U-turn he sped back in the direction from which he'd come. The blips strengthened slightly. A roadsign on the left pointed to Nonancourt. Samson took a chance and turned left. He was rewarded by an increased strength of reception.

Even at night it was evident that Nonancourt, situated at the extreme south of Normandy, had escaped much of the twentieth century's industrial corrosion. Timbered medieval houses proudly abutted the town's central market place and as Samson drove slowly, gradually narrowing the point of contact between himself and the Jaguar, he wondered what purpose Winstanley had in coming to a place marked on his road-map in the smallest print.

It was on the edge of the town by the banks of the river Avre that the blips increased almost to maximum intensity. Samson brought the Granada to a halt in the shadow of a plane tree by a small bridge. He climbed out and looked around. On the far side of the river he saw the Jaguar parked beside four other cars near a large house which was approached by a short, well-illuminated drive. A roughly cut grass lawn sloped down from the house to the river.

After pausing momentarily to gaze down at the gently flowing river Samson walked across the bridge. In a town such as Nonancourt a collector of old books might find some treasures and it occurred to him that the house might be the home of an antiquarian bookseller. After checking that no one was in sight he hurried across the lawn and vanished into shadows. From here, keeping close to an ornamental hedge, he made his way up to the house. All the ground-floor windows were shuttered but cracks of light and a man's braying laugh showed the place was occupied. Samson could just hear the hum of voices. Then a dog barked and the voices became silent.

Although he sometimes regarded the maxim 'Discretion is the better part of valour' as a cowardly mandate to cop-out, Samson saw no virtue in prolonging his trespass. He was recrossing the bridge when the front door of the house opened. A man's silhouette and a large dog's outline were framed against interior light. Samson increased his pace and was glad to reach his car. He had no wish to measure his courage against the aggression of a big guard dog. He waited until man and dog went indoors before starting the car engine.

On his way through the town he had noticed a small hotel. He decided to go there. The time had come to make some enquiries. He hoped his quarry wouldn't disappear while he was having a much-needed drink.

Gravel crunched under car tyres as he came to a halt in

51

a courtyard beside the hotel. There was only one other car in the park, an old Simca. Samson drove past it to a high wall which was in shadow.

The hotel looked provincially French, about a-hundred-and-fifty years old, and when he entered the creaking outer door he was greeted by the redolence of garlic. He walked through an antechamber where mustard wallpaper clashed violently with a patterned carpet to where a grey-haired woman sat in a cubby-hole. She had the faded looks of someone prematurely aged by worry and was evidently the receptionist. She looked up as Samson approached.

In his best French (which in the past had sometimes caused him to be mistaken for a Dutchman) he enquired whether there was a bar. She indicated a nearby doorway. He went through into a small bar where a few men were drinking. His arrival was marked by a brief lull in conversation and a moment later the receptionist appeared behind the bar. She evidently doubled as barmaid.

He ordered a large whisky and looked around. The other customers were middle-aged except for one good-looking and slightly effeminate young man who, when he caught Samson's eye, smiled.

As he paid for the drink Samson asked the receptionist/barmaid if many foreign tourists came to Nonancourt.

'We see a few.'

'Does the town have a long history?'

After wrinkling a striated upper lip the woman nodded towards the young man. 'You should ask him. He's a schoolmaster and knows everything about Nonancourt.'

The man in question detached himself from two others and came across to Samson. He was accompanied by an after-shave which smelled of lilies of the valley. 'I overheard that,' he said in near-perfect English. 'You aren't by any chance from Earls Colne?'

'Earls Colne?'

'It is in Essex. We in Nonancourt are twinned with Earls Colne.'

'No. I'm from London.'

'Ah.' The young man looked disappointed. 'We have exchange visits,' he said.

'I'm just passing through,' said Samson. 'You have a lovely town. I was down by the river a few minutes ago. A lovely scene.'

The young man smiled. 'It is lovely,' he said. 'May I introduce myself. I'm Jean-Pierre Corot but, before you ask, no, I am not related to the great artist.'

'My name is Samson and, so far as I know, I'm not related to the strong man who didn't care much for barbers.'

Corot's eyebrows became a circumflex. 'Barbers?'

'*Les barbiers*,' said Samson.

Corot laughed. 'I understand. As in *Il barbiere di Siviglia*.' He held out his hand. 'I am pleased to meet you, Mr Rossini.'

The woman behind the bar laughed. It was obvious that she understood English.

Samson wanted information, not cross-talk. He said, 'Can I get you a drink? What would you like?'

'That is truly *entente cordiale*. Yes, I would like a Pernod.'

While the barmaid was getting the drink Samson said, 'Your town must have seen much history.'

'Indeed, yes. Every house has a story to tell. A little way from here there is a hotel which was once a post-house. In 1715 the wife of the postmaster, Suzanne de la Cour, saved from ambush James the Third Stuart who was journeying to England to reconquer his throne.'

'How sad the attempt failed,' said Samson who cared nothing for Jacobite aspirations. He handed the barmaid a twenty franc note and, passing the glass of Pernod to the schoolmaster, went on, 'Before I came in here I took a walk by the river. There's a large house by the bridge. Is it a public building?'

The question seemed to unsettle Corot. He shuffled his feet, looked down at his glass of Pernod as if scrutinising the cloudy liquid for some cryptic message, and then glanced up at the clock on the wall.

'Public building? No. . . . My God, is that the time!'

Samson was aware that the bar had become very quiet and, out of the corner of his eye, saw the barmaid disappear in the direction of the adjoining cubby-hole. It was plain that he had asked an unwanted question. He tried to change the subject. 'Does this town have a mayor?' he asked.

Eyes flickering around like someone in search of an escape route from an invincible bore, Corot replied grudgingly, 'Yes.'

'What, approximately, is the population of Nonancourt?'

'The population? About nine thousand, I think.'

Corot drained the Pernod and placed the empty glass on the bar counter. 'You must excuse me, I shall be late. My friend would never forgive me. We are due to set off on holiday this very night.'

With a wave of his hand, and *À bientot* to the others in the bar, Corot hurried away leaving Samson to finish his whisky and wonder why his question about the house by the bridge had been a *faux pas*.

After finishing his drink he left the bar and went to the receptionist's cubby-hole. She was speaking on the telephone but when he appeared she made a quick farewell and put down the 'phone. 'Can I help you?' she asked.

Samson leaned forward with a confidential air. 'I was only passing through your delightful town on my way to the south but I've half a mind to spend the night here, that is, if there are shops which sell old books. Antiquarian bookshops. That's my line of business, you see.'

'There is a bookshop at the end of the Grande Rue. They sell a few second-hand books. Inexpensive books.'

'Old books?'

The worry-lines etched on her forehead deepened. 'Not exactly old. Well used.'

Samson looked doubtful. 'That's not quite what I had in mind. When I asked Monsieur Corot about the house by the bridge I was wondering if it might be a museum or a library.'

She shook her head.

'A private house?' Samson pursued.

The receptionist glanced around as though fearful of being overheard. 'I believe so,' she said.

'The mayor's house perhaps?'

She shook her head, and then, 'Would monsieur be staying here tonight? I have rooms available.'

'No. I must be on my way.'

'A meal maybe. Something to eat?' A note of urgency had entered her voice as though her job depended on successfully soliciting custom.

Samson hesitated. He was hungry but he didn't know how long his quarry would be staying at Nonancourt and he knew he should be returning to his car. During his moment of indecision she reached for a menu and handed it to him. 'I can assure you that you will be well satisfied with our cuisine.'

The temptation to read the menu was irresistible. Samson's gastric juices were instantly stimulated.

'The *Longe de Porc à la Normande* is very good,' she said. 'It is served with a cream *sauce Normande*.'

'Sounds good.'

'With a wine of the region,' she went on. 'We have a very good cellar.'

He put down the menu and looked at pale grey eyes which begged him to stay for a meal. 'The price is very reasonable,' she said.

A sort of desperation had entered her voice as though she would be punished if she couldn't persuade him to dine in the hotel restaurant. Samson felt he was being importuned and began to suspect she might be under orders to detain him. But, if so, who had given the orders? He remembered Corot's change of attitude when the house by the bridge had been mentioned and how the schoolmaster had made an excuse to leave, and how the receptionist had avoided his query about the ownership of the house and switched to talking about the possibility of him staying the night.

'I'm sure the price is reasonable,' he said, 'but I must be going.'

He turned to leave.

'Monsieur would be well-satisfied with the service – all services,' she wailed after him almost as though she was offering a service more personal and intimate than the provision of an excellent meal.

He didn't reply, but hurried out to where his car was parked. As he approached he saw a pair of trousered legs protruding from under the vehicle. Stooping down, he grabbed ankles and hauled. The response was a muffled oath and a kicking of legs.

Samson pulled his catch clear of the car. It was a young curly haired man wearing a shabby *blouson*. As the man tried to scramble to his feet Samson pushed him back and sank down on him, straddling his stomach. Pressure of weight made the other gasp.

In accented French Samson asked, 'What were you doing to my car?'

'A thousand pardons. A mistake . . .'

'A very big mistake. Who told you to— ' The sentence was never finished. Something hard and heavy hit the back of Samson's head and he blacked out, but in the split-second between blow and oblivion he caught the smell of lilies of the valley.

He came to and sat up. The courtyard was still empty apart from the old Simca. Probing the back of his head with his fingers he felt a bump, but the skin hadn't been broken. As he staggered to his feet he noticed a dark stain on the shadowy gravel surface of the courtyard. Something was seeping from the underside of his car.

Although he had given Mrs Huntingdon-Winstanley the impression that he had little knowledge of automobiles he had become proficient in the know-how of car mechanics ever since a case when he had been obliged to consult an engineer to find out how to make a pall of smoke come out of the exhaust pipe at the press of a button. He was too bulky to squeeze under the car but he knew that the fluid spreading across the gravel was either oil or fluid from the hydraulic brake system. It was a simple enough job for any car mechanic to slacken off the pipe union nut and fluid would squirt out. The previous investigator called Brightwell had been killed when the brakes on his car had failed.

The courtyard was level; it would be easy to check whether the brakes worked. Samson got into the car, started the engine and moved forward very slowly. He pressed the brake pedal; there was no response. The car drifted to a halt brought to inertia by the operation of friction. Whether he liked it or not he was now stranded in Nonancourt and would lose the men he was pursuing. And, like it or not, he would be obliged to stay the night.

Angry with himself for having lost a few minutes in finishing his whisky, and relaxing after the long drive, he tried to work out how anyone could have known of his presence in this obscure town. Had he himself been followed? Or had Corot been acting on someone's orders?

He got out of the car, locked the door, and made his way back to the hotel.

The grey-haired receptionist looked up as he walked towards her cubby-hole. Her lips parted but not in a smile.

'I've changed my mind,' he said. 'I'd like a meal and a room for the night.'

'A room for the night?' She repeated the phrase with an air of incredulity.

'Yes, a room for the night.'

With trembling hands she reached for a ledger with frayed edges. Opening the ledger she glanced down and said, 'I fear I made a mistake, a terrible mistake, when I spoke to you earlier. I thought we had rooms available, but find we have none.' She closed the ledger. 'I apologise.'

Samson didn't move. 'While I was in here having a drink,' he said, 'someone was tampering with my car.'

The receptionist reached out and placed her hand on a bell-push. The action seemed to increase her confidence because in a firmer voice she said, 'The hotel management has no responsibility for cars belonging to customers. They are parked at the customer's own risk.'

'I didn't say my car was parked here. What makes you think it is? And what else do you know?'

'I assume it's here. It's forbidden to park in the street.'

Her hand was hovering over the bell-push and he guessed she was ready to ring for help. His head was aching and he wasn't in the mood for argument or to advertise his presence more widely.

'You're right,' he said, 'it is in the hotel car park, and it'll have to remain there until I can get someone to attend to it. In the meanwhile I shall have to stay in this town.'

'There's a very good hotel down the road,' she said quickly. '*Le Grand Cerf*. I'm sure they'll have a vacancy and they have a good restaurant also.'

He nodded towards the bell-push. 'You won't need to use that. I'm going now.' He paused. 'Just one other thing. Can you tell me where Monsieur Corot lives?'

'I'm sorry, I don't know.'

'Does he live alone? Is he married or single?'

She turned her head away to avoid meeting his eyes. 'I know nothing about him except that he is a teacher, and the school is closed, and he is on holiday.'

'He said something about going on holiday with a friend. Have you any idea where he's going?'

She didn't reply.

'Good night, madame,' said Samson, and he walked out of the hotel.

After booking in at the hotel *Le Grand Cerf* he went on foot to the river. It was a mild April evening and he passed a number of people out for a stroll. One young couple paused every few paces to exchange kisses and Samson, who had never been lucky in love, experienced an unexpected moment of compassion. In his professional and personal experience falling in love was more often than not a descent into a pit of disillusion. Perhaps some fortunate men and women loved and won a lifetime happiness but they didn't come his way.

He watched the lovers, still kissing, disappear along the river bank before crossing the bridge. The cars outside the house had disappeared. Winstanley and Robert Mansour had done their business, whatever that was, and gone.

He didn't often feel depressed but he felt depressed now. His car had been immobilised, he had failed to keep track of his quarry and, out of the blue, he had been reminded of the fragility of human relationships. He walked rapidly back to *Le Grand Cerf*. There was nothing a strong whisky and an appetising meal wouldn't put right.

That night he slept badly and dreamed of a woman he had known twenty years before who had said, with a cruel laugh, 'I'll bet they called you "Fatty" at school. You're gross! You revolt me!'

After a light breakfast of croissants and strong coffee he tried to put through a long distance call to his office. He needed to inform Shandy of the situation. But after a long delay the operator told him the number was unobtainable.

Samson tried another number which belonged to a

woman who lived alone in a flat above the office. That too was unobtainable. An English operator told him, 'There seems to be a fault on the line. It'll be reported.'

In his haste to leave England he had overlooked the advisability of belonging to an organisation which provided an overseas breakdown service but for the first time since arriving in Nonancourt luck was on his side. Within a few minutes of booking out of the hotel he found a garage willing to repair the car's braking system.

While waiting for the service to be completed he called in at an estate agent's office where he presented himself as a potential client for a holiday home in the area. He said he wanted a large house where he could entertain guests, preferably in or near a town and preferably close to a river as his hobby was the study of insect life on waterways.

The agent, a man with pencil moustache and red polka-dot bow tie, said he had nothing on his books at the present which exactly fitted these requirements but—

Samson interrupted a flow of useless alternatives by saying, 'There's a house by the bridge which would suit me well.' A few sentences later, having established the precise location of the house the agent said, 'Unfortunately that house is not for sale, nor is it likely to be.' Samson said he'd be willing to make an offer, a substantial offer, to the owner, whoever he might be. . . . 'Who is he, by the way?'

'I know little about him except that he is a doctor and said to be expert in certain types of surgery.'

'What types of surgery?'

'The surgery which women have to delay the onset of age.'

'Cosmetic surgery?'

'I expect so.'

'What's his name?'

'Maurice. That's his second name. I don't know the first.'

'And how old is this Doctor Maurice?'

A change came over the agent. He was experienced enough to recognise the difference between a potential client and a time-waster. 'If you will kindly leave your name and address I will personally see that details of any properties similar to your requirements are sent to you.'

In his turn Samson was experienced enough to recognise when a line of enquiry was exhausted. He had no intention of providing his name and address. He said, 'That won't be necessary,' favoured the agent with a grateful smile and walked away.

His next call was at the post office where he looked through a telephone directory. There was no one listed under the name of 'Maurice'.

Before collecting his car he again tried to contact Shandy. The number was still unobtainable.

At the garage he struck up a conversation with a mechanic by asking about local trade. He said that on the previous evening, while out for a stroll, he had noticed a number of expensive cars parked outside a house by the bridge. If all these came for servicing business must be good.

The mechanic shook his head. 'I don't know about that. The owner isn't a native of Nonancourt. He's a foreigner who arrived only a few years ago. I believe he was once married to a French woman but they got divorced. He never comes here except occasionally for gas. Where his cars are serviced, I don't know.'

Samson paid the bill and set off for le Touquet only to find on arrival that no flights were available. He then drove to Boulogne. At the quayside he was told that there were delays to car ferries owing to adverse weather in the Channel.

By now, thoroughly fed up, he tried again to contact Shandy. His office number was still unobtainable but when he called her home number her husband, Paul, answered.

'Shandy isn't here,' he said. 'I think she's still trying to salvage things.'

'Salvage? What salvage?'

'Haven't you heard? Your office was burned down last night.'

Chapter 5

He spent the night at a hotel in Boulogne and, on the following day, weather conditions having improved, he boarded a ferry. After disembarking at Dover he drove straight to his office arriving just before midday. The entrance to the premises was sandwiched between a bookmaker's shop and a mini-supermarket run by an Indian family. The bookmaker's had been boarded up and, looking up, he saw the window of his office had been smashed and the brickwork was darkly stained.

He went through the entrance, hurried down a narrow corridor and up uncarpeted stairs which led to another corridor. A brown door which led into his office hung listlessly on its hinges. As he went through he saw Shandy bending over an open drawer in a metal filing cabinet. Her back was to him and she jerked upright when he spoke her name.

'You made me jump. Thank God you're back. Paul told me about your call.'

He looked around the fire-wrecked room which bore the ravages of damp from fire hydrants as well as the charred remains of furnishings.

'What a mess,' he said.

'Your room isn't quite so bad,' she replied, 'but it's bad enough. I've managed to salvage some of the reference books but most have been damaged or destroyed.'

Samson went to the door which led to his room and

glanced inside. It appeared that more damage had been inflicted by hydrants than by fire. He returned to Shandy. 'Tell me exactly what happened. Paul didn't seem to know too much and I got the impression that the whole building had gone up in flames.' He noticed a telephone perched on a makeshift table. 'Is that working?'

'We've been reconnected. It's business as usual. Like the Windmill, we never close. But the electric ring isn't working. The cable from the plug got burned and I haven't replaced it yet.' She picked up a thermos flask. 'Like a nice hot coffee while I tell you the story?'

'Thanks.'

She poured a measure of coffee into a plastic cup and passed it to him.

'It was Miss Trimble who raised the alarm,' she said, referring to the woman who lived above the office. 'She was working late a couple of nights ago embroidering a table cloth when she smelled smoke. She went down and saw smoke seeping out under the door. She raced upstairs and dialled 999 but her 'phone wasn't working. Luckily she didn't panic and ran next door to where Mr Kirmani was just packing up for the night. The fire engine arrived within ten minutes and the men managed to contain the blaze before it took full hold.'

'Any idea how it started?'

'I was coming to that. Miss Trimble rang me and I went round at once. The police came but there was nothing much they could do at the time but the next morning, yesterday morning, the CID were round asking questions. And the Forensic came along. The long and short of it is that they suspect arson. The fire could have been started by someone pushing a petrol-soaked rag through the letter-box and then dropping a lighted match, or some other form of ignition.'

Samson put down an empty coffee cup and went across to the smashed window to look out at the scene below. The street seemed unusually noisy with its bustle of pedestrians and heavy flow of motorised traffic. On the opposite side of the street the nesting pigeon was preening itself while perched on a gutter.

He turned to Shandy. 'Any theories as to who might have done it?'

'One of the Kirmani children remembers seeing a man come out of the entrance and hurry away at around ten-thirty in the evening which must have been about the time the fire started. She's given a description to the police. For a ten-year-old it's pretty good. . . . Medium height, rather thin, short fair hair, caucasian, bad complexion, wearing black bomber jacket, jeans and sneakers.'

For a moment Samson looked like a man weighed down by all the imponderables in the universe. Then he straightened his back and lifted his head. 'It's a good description,' he said. 'It could fit the guy who came at me with a knife the night I went out for a meal in Soho.'

'You wondered if he was someone in Winstanley's pay or just a common mugger.' She went to the annexe which housed a sink. As she swilled out the thermos flask she said, 'I've put in an insurance claim and the assessor is coming this afternoon.'

Samson gave a slight smile. 'I'm glad the clocks had been moved. They were under-insured. But what about the equipment and papers?'

'You're lucky to have an efficient secretary who clears her desk each evening and files everything safely away. The cabinets got scorched, as you can see, but they resisted. Some of the hardware got damaged though. My word-processor is on the blink and the Fax is pretty sick.'

'It seems an amateurish job,' said Samson. 'A professional would have broken in, taken anything he might have wanted, and then set fire to the place from the inside.'

Shandy nodded and the lock of hair fell over her forehead. Brushing it back she said, 'I've been very patient. But I'm dying to know. How did you get on?'

Samson told her of his trip, of how he followed the Jaguar to Nonancourt, of the cars parked near the house by the bridge, of the cool reception at the first hotel, of his car being sabotaged, and of his subsequent enquiries which revealed that a cosmetic surgeon called Maurice lived at the house.

Shandy looked puzzled. 'Why should a man like Winstanley, or this Robert guy, call on a cosmetic surgeon?' she asked.

'That's what I've been asking myself,' Samson replied, 'unless Winstanley was a patient. He looks remarkably well-preserved. VSOP in fact. Talking of which— ' He broke off to return to his own room. Shandy followed. 'Thank God,' he said, 'at least *that* didn't go up in smoke.' He crossed a damp carpet to a teak cocktail cabinet and opened it. 'I think I'll have a brandy. Would you like one?'

'No, thanks. You were saying?'

'Yes, I was mentioning Winstanley's appearance.' Samson spoke slowly as he poured brandy into a whisky tumbler. 'I'd be surprised if he'd had any surgery. I had a good look at him and I think he's simply someone who inherited a favourable genetic code. A few men – not me, alas – seem to improve with age and that's nothing to do with a so-called healthy life. It's chance thrown up by millions of years of natural selection.'

'But Mrs H-W wasn't so lucky in the evolutionary stakes according to your description of her.'

'That's right. It can cause envy or jealousy in a marriage if one partner ages noticeably more than the other.' He took a sip of brandy. 'I can't see any connection between cosmetic surgery and an interest in collecting antiquarian books, can you?'

Before Shandy could answer the 'phone rang in her

room. She answered it and when she returned she looked amused. 'It's a case of talk of the devil,' she said. 'Mrs H-W is on the line and insists on speaking to you.'

'How the hell did she know I was back?'

Shandy shrugged. 'Search me.'

Samson went to the makeshift table and picked up the handset. 'Samson here,' he said.

'Mr Samson, I want to see you. Will you come round?'

'How did you know I was back?'

An audible expulsion of breath came down the line. 'I'm not prepared to answer questions on the telephone. Will you, or will you not, come and see me?'

'I'll come, but later. I've other matters to attend to.'

'When? I don't like being put off.'

Samson mentally added a few pounds to the bill he would ultimately present. It would come under the head of 'Sundries' but more accurately should be labelled 'For aggravation suffered'.

'Some time after five o'clock,' he said. 'Goodbye, Mrs Huntingdon-Winstanley.'

The maid, Jennifer, showed him into the stuffy sitting room. He noticed that the furs had been removed from draping the furniture. Otherwise, the room was exactly the same. A pile of spillikins and a pack of playing cards were on the walnut table like two teams waiting to be chosen for play.

Mrs Huntingdon-Winstanley made a limping entrance like a grand duchess and it was easy to imagine a row of ghostly courtiers bowing their heads as she passed.

'You're late,' she said. 'It's after seven.'

'I've had a lot to attend to.'

'That's no excuse.'

She made her way to the table and the maid quietly closed the door.

'Sit down, Mr Samson.'

When she was seated and the stick resting against her chair she said, 'Now then, you asked me a question: How did I know you were back. I'll tell you. Simon called me from somewhere in France to say he thought you would be. He was crowing with triumph. It was galling. I expected better of you.' Her bright blue eyes bored into him. 'How do you account for your blundering? I'll tell you now. You won't be paid for making mistakes.'

Samson wasn't often put at a disadvantage by a client but he felt disadvantaged and angry.

'Am I to understand that your husband knew – and knew from you – that he was being followed?'

'Of course he knew, but I didn't tell him.' She picked up a spillikin stick. 'Come on, I'll play you. How about a stake of a thousand pounds or is that too much for you?'

For two pins or a couple of spillikin tokens Samson would have left there and then but, not only was he intrigued by the eccentric old woman, he had a score to repay for his wounded pride.

'You're on,' he said, 'provided I know the rules in advance. I don't want them made up during the game. And I shall expect honest answers to the questions I shall ask.'

'Honest answers,' she said indignantly. 'I'm not a liar!'

'Glad to hear it.'

She picked up a spillikin stick and tapped it on the table like a conductor on a rostrum about to lead an orchestra into a symphony concert.

'You score one for every spillikin you remove without disturbing the others,' she said. 'But if through clumsiness you disturb them you lose a point. For example, if you take one but in so doing you move the others, you lose a point. Is that clear?'

'Perfectly.'

'There are thirty-nine in the pile, exactly the number of the articles of faith of the Church of England and exactly half of a full pack of Tarot cards. The number gives the game a certain mystique, don't you think?' She reached into her handbag and brought out a slim, gold ballpoint pen. 'I'll keep the score,' she said. 'I'll let you start and that's giving you an advantage but it's the only concession I'll make. Go on. Start.'

Samson hooked at the replica of a scallop shell and landed it safely.

Mrs Huntingdon-Winstanley then reached out. Her hand trembled but she managed to extract a minute camel. 'That's getting a camel with the eye of a needle, as I like to say,' she remarked.

Samson rose from his chair and walked round the table surveying the pile of spillikins from all angles.

'Ha,' she exclaimed. 'You're learning fast.'

Without taking his eyes off the spillikins he said, 'How did your husband know all about my movements? Are you sure you didn't tell him I was going to follow?'

'I didn't have to tell him anything. He learned for himself. Perhaps Jennifer was listening to me but I can't prove it. Or he may have had my telephone tapped. It's part of the fun of trying to outwit each other. It keeps us young.'

'You make it sound like a game,' said Samson, still studying the spillikin pile.

'Of course it's a game. All life is a game, Mr Samson.'

Samson had heard this cliché before. It was spoken by people who wanted to avoid looking below the surface of their own lives for fear of what they might find.

'So you think it was your maid,' he said, 'or a tapped telephone.'

'I didn't say that. You're jumping to conclusions. I said perhaps Jennifer was listening; perhaps the telephone was tapped; but it was something else. . . . Hurry up. If you take longer than two minutes you forfeit the game. And that isn't a made-up rule.'

Samson reached out and delicately hooked the end of his ivory stick into the hole of a little discus at the top of the pile. He slowly extracted it and laid it on the table.

'What was the "something else"?' he asked.

'The something else? Oh, yes. After your visit to the underground garage Robert examined the car and found some sort of radio contrivance you'd secreted in the boot. They decided to leave it and allow you to follow them. They knew, all the time, that they were being followed.'

'When did you find that out?'

'Simon told me when he was crowing.'

Her hand wavered as she pulled out a top hat. The pile trembled and a piece fell. 'Damn,' she said. 'That's one up to you. I must be losing my touch.'

'I'm still not clear how they knew I was at Nonancourt.'

'Simple. Simon was calling on a friend at his private home and, while he was with him, Robert remained outside hiding behind some bushes. He spotted you.'

Samson leaned forward and studied the pile of spillikins with the concentration of a chess grand master.

'Do you need a magnifying glass?' asked Mrs Huntingdon-Winstanley sarcastically. 'Where is your magnifying glass, by the way? I thought all you sleuths carried magnifying glasses.'

Samson ignored the jibe. 'I don't understand how they knew where I was,' he said. 'They may have known I was following at a distance but they couldn't have known whether or not I'd end up with them in Nonancourt. I could easily have missed the turning and gone out of range. And how did they find out where my car was parked?'

'I can't answer all that but Simon did say Robert hid behind some bushes and spotted you.'

'And got someone to tamper with my car?'

'I don't know about that. Hurry up. It's your move. This is exciting, isn't it?'

Having studied the pile Samson removed the replica of a throne.

'You've now scored three to my one,' she said. 'I shall have to try harder.' She stretched out her arm and gingerly tried to pull out a hunting horn. At the last moment the pile began to shiver. She stopped but it was too late. Two pieces fell. 'Damn, double damn,' she said.

'Mrs Huntingdon-Winstanley, did you know that your husband's friend at Nonancourt is a surgeon and his name is Maurice?'

She looked up from her scoring pad. 'How do you know he's a surgeon?'

'I made enquiries. He specialises in cosmetic surgery. Have you any idea why your husband should call on someone who specialises in cosmetic surgery?'

A cloud seemed to pass over her bright blue eyes. 'I've no idea . . . Unless . . . Simon knows I'm worried about my appearance. I just wonder if he was seeking some sort of help for me. Do you think that might be the explanation?'

'It may be. But there could be other explanations. I'd have to continue working on the case if you really want to know what the explanation is. Do you want me to carry on?'

While he was speaking she had taken a handkerchief from her handbag and was blowing her nose. 'Excuse me,' she said. 'When he said he was visiting a friend I assumed it was a contact in the book business. But I'm touched to think he might have been visiting a surgeon on my account.' She put the handkerchief away. 'But of course I want you to carry on. One mustn't be deceived by sentiment, particularly if it might turn out to be false sentiment. I shan't say a word to him. Besides, the game goes on. One of us must win and I'm determined it shan't be him. That doesn't mean I don't care for him. I care deeply. But enough of that. It's your turn.'

Samson regarded the pile. It was obvious that once a player got near the bottom of the pile it would become easier to lift pieces without risk of dislodging any. The skill in manipulation was most important in the early stages.

He extracted a miniature Eiffel Tower.

71

'You're still winning,' she said. 'I'll have to do something about that.'

With shaking hand she probed at the top token.

Samson glanced at his watch. 'I thought there was a time limit,' he said.

'Don't be a rotten sport.'

Eventually she removed the top piece of a shrinking pyramid but her probings had made it impossible for Samson to find an available hole as a tiny cup had been turned so that its handle was buried.

'Get out of that,' she said.

'When are you expecting your husband back?'

'I don't know. He'll just turn up. Maybe in three days, maybe in ten. I'll let you know when his next trip to France has been arranged.'

'And no doubt, if I follow, he'll know I'm following.' Samson shook his head. 'It seems a pointless exercise but if you want to throw your money away, that's up to you.'

'It's not pointless,' she said. 'It's cat and mouse. Fun. Haven't you got a sense of fun? Go on, it's your move.'

Samson wasn't sure whether she was casting him in the role of the cat or the mouse. He gazed at the pile. 'You've set me a problem,' he said. 'I can't get at any of the pieces.'

'If you can't go, you forfeit the game. You must try, Mr Samson, even if it means knocking some of the spillikins over.'

Holding up his spillikin stick he said, 'Just refresh my memory. I must use this to lift out a piece. I can't use my fingers, only this stick. Is that right?'

'Quite correct.'

'So long as only this stick is used I'm entitled to take any piece provided the pile isn't disturbed.'

She gave him a suspicious look. 'I don't know what you're driving at. I've made myself perfectly plain.'

'Perfectly,' he said and he snapped the stick in two.

She was aghast. 'What do you think you're doing?'

72

'I'll show you.' With half a stick in each hand Samson was able to lever the cup from the top of the pile. 'I've only used this stick,' he said.

'You've cheated!' She threw down her own stick and, like a sulky child, said, 'I'm not playing any more. The game is over. And you needn't think you've won, because you haven't. It's null and void. So there!'

Samson stooped down and picked up his briefcase. 'Not only is the game null and void, Mrs Huntingdon-Winstanley, but so is your assignment. I'm withdrawing from the case. Your initial payment doesn't quite meet my fees and out-of-pocket disbursements and so I shall be sending a further account.'

As he began moving towards the door she cried out, 'Wait!' He paused. 'Yes?'

'I'm ashamed. Very ashamed. But I haven't been entirely honest with you. Please come and sit down.'

The plea in her voice was reinforced by the anguish of her features. The cracks in her face had been papered over by make-up but now the paper looked torn and frayed. Her shoulders were bowed and she seemed physically to have shrunk.

'I've no one to turn to,' she went on, 'except people who are paid for their services. Please don't desert me. I'll tell the truth, I promise.'

Samson was in a dilemma, uncertain whether to follow his business acumen or to defer to common sense. Business acumen said she was a client with apparently unlimited resources which she was prepared to squander; common sense told him he could find himself in an unacceptable degree of danger and it would be better to forego making a handsome profit.

Business acumen won. He returned to the table and sat down. 'I'm listening,' he said.

She swallowed, and when she spoke her voice had lost its strident arrogance.

73

'I've misled you, Mr Samson. It's not the women I'm worried about. So long as he keeps his affairs out of the way I don't mind at all. Not that he has all that many.' Her voice became almost inaudible. 'To be absolutely frank I think he enjoys the company of his own sex as much as that of the opposite sex. No, it's not that aspect which troubles me.'

She paused and Samson asked, 'Why did you tell me that you wanted evidence of his womanising – what he got up to – if that wasn't the case?'

'It's a long story.'

'I'm still listening.'

'I've told you some lies.'

'I realise that.'

'Whoppers.'

'Go on.'

Eyes downcast as any humble penitent she began, 'The first whopper was telling you my company had outlets to major stores which sold costume jewellery, that the company had been founded by my grandfather, and that Simon was a salesman. I did own a boutique which sold such artefacts after Simon's father died, and I did acquire two others which between the three provided an income. These are run by managers but it isn't a big concern as I pretended.'

She looked up quickly as if to gauge his reaction to this confession.

'What has your husband's father to do with all this?' he asked.

She sighed. 'Well, you see, I was never in business. I was a nurse. I worked for a short while in the NHS and then I went into the private sector. In that sphere I got a job nursing a sick old man who was quite rich. Simon's father. I was a good nurse although I say so myself. He was terminally ill and I would sit up all night with him letting him talk about his achievements and the empire he'd built up. He was a furrier. His company made fur coats, stoles and

74

the like. But that's digressing. The point is that he made a will leaving everything to me.'

'What about Simon?' Samson intervened.

'He got nothing. James, his father, cut him out of an earlier will after a terrible quarrel over money. The problem was that Simon didn't see why, having a rich father, he should work. Naturally he contested the will. His barrister talked about "undue influence" on my part, but my barrister was able to show there had been no undue influence and that James had been quite *compos mentis* when he made the will. I believe the law might have since been changed with regard to inheritance provisions but at that time I received the whole estate.'

She paused, waiting for him to ask inevitable questions.

'How did you come to marry Simon? Are you really married to him?'

'Yes, I am.' She gave another sigh. 'Although I was nursing the father I fell in love with the son. I was potty about him and when, after he lost the case about the will, he came up to me and said, "There are no hard feelings; I do really care about you", and as proof handed me a single red rose, I succumbed against my better instincts. He worked on me. I knew he was working on me but I was incapable of resisting. In the end I married him. Against every sensible instinct I settled a deed which entitled him to a regular income. He said he needed to have a degree of independence if he was to feel a man. I swallowed that. It wasn't a large allowance but now he doesn't seem so dependent on it. I think he's getting money from elsewhere.'

Again she paused to assess Samson's reactions.

'I understand you so far, but why are you Huntingdon-Winstanley when he seems to be Winstanley?'

'Huntingdon was my maiden name. I was Nurse Huntingdon. It may seem odd to you but part of the arrangement, or the deal as people would say nowadays, was that I kept my name even if it was added to his.' Her eyes misted with reminiscence. 'After he proposed we went on a world tour to celebrate and we got married in the Seychelles.'

'He was never Simon Smith?'

'No. That was an untruth.'

'My next question', said Samson, 'may seem impertinent but you don't strike me as someone obliged to work for a living. Was nursing purely a vocational career?'

She managed to straighten bent shoulders. 'My family was distinguished, if impoverished,' she said, 'and anyway I like looking after people. I'd love to look after Simon if he'd allow me. Or I would have done. This arthritis— '

She appeared to be on the verge of tears and Samson changed his line of questioning. 'If you aren't bothered about other women, what does trouble you?'

'If I told you, you'd probably think it was the nonsensical ramblings of a stupid old woman.'

Her tearful self-pity had suddenly vanished and she was now looking coyly at him as if expecting a gallant denial of the self-depreciation.

'What does trouble you?' he repeated.

Before replying she glanced around and then she leaned forward and crooked a beckoning finger. Samson inched closer to the table.

'I'm afraid he might be involved in something illegal,' she whispered.

'What makes you think that?'

'I told you that I'd employed another detective before you.'

'Brightwell?'

'Yes, Brightwell. Before his unfortunate death he had been observing the movements of Simon and Robert here in London. One morning, it was a cold day in February and we'd had a sharp fall of snow, everywhere was very bleak, Robert parked the car near Hyde Park and then got out and went for a stroll, leaving Simon in the car. I'm not surprised. If you knew Simon as I do, you'd know he was the last man to want to go for a walk on a freezing winter day. Brightwell followed Robert and saw him meet another man near the Albert Memorial. Together they went back to the car. They got in and all three talked for a bit. Then the man got out. Simon and Robert drove off and Brightwell followed the man.'

She paused, allowing Samson to assimilate the story so far. 'You're with me?' she asked.

'I'm with you.'

'Good. I don't like having to repeat myself. But you were looking a little detached, as though your mind was elsewhere.'

In a sense Samson had been elsewhere. She was still speaking softly and he had been trying to adjust his concealed tape-recorder without her noticing. 'You have all my attention,' he said.

'Well then, Brightwell followed this other man. He wanted to see where he went and to get a good look at him. This fellow hailed a taxi and sped away in it. Brightwell couldn't follow but he'd managed to get close enough to the man and . . . what do you think?'

'I don't know what to think,' said Samson dutifully.

'Brightwell recognised him as a gangland figure, someone with a reputation for violence' – she dropped her voice to a whisper once more – 'a killer! Brightwell said he was a "contract man" and would kill for money. He said he was fairly sure he was a man on the run who had emigrated to Spain. He must have slipped back into this country. I was horrified. I could hardly believe my ears. Why on earth should Simon want to associate with such a person?'

An immediate answer came to Samson but he said, 'Did you ask Brightwell that question?'

'I did, and what do you think he said?'

'He probably advised you to take precautions for your own safety.'

She seemed surprised. 'So you think the same as he. That's because you don't know Simon as well as I do. I'm perfectly certain he wouldn't do anything to harm me. We've had some bad moments, admittedly, but surely he must still care for me a little. He always remembers my birthday and brings back presents from abroad.'

Samson was familiar with the effects of self-deception. When emotionally involved, people could blind themselves to the obvious; it was a protection against unbearable reality. He knew Mrs Huntingdon-Winstanley wouldn't be easily convinced that she might be a hit-man's target. And yet when she had telephoned him at his flat she had said something about dying in suspicious circumstances and he had replied that she could rest assured that he would investigate if this should happen.

'Did Brightwell say anything else apart from taking precautions for your own safety? Did he have any theories why your husband should be meeting this man, and did he tell you the man's name?'

'He hadn't got any theories, so far as I know, and he did tell me the name but for the life of me I can't remember it. It was a common or garden name like Bloggs or Chuck, a one-syllable name.'

'How long after this encounter with Bloggs or Chuck did Brightwell have his fatal accident?'

'Only a week or so. It was on a dangerous bend in Hampshire. I didn't hear about it until I 'phoned his office a few days after. Have you got any idea why Simon should be associating with such a man apart from the notion that he might be wanting to do me in which, frankly, I don't believe.'

'Have you made a will?'

'Of course.'

'Is your husband the principal beneficiary?'

She sat up very straight and in a voice which was far from a whisper said, 'That's none of your business!'

'If you want my help it's very much my business.'

She looked disgruntled and again he was reminded of

a child, a child that has had its wrist slightly slapped.

'All right,' she said, 'if you must know, he is the main beneficiary, but not the only one. I have charities which I endow.'

'Nevertheless, he would benefit by your death.'

'To some extent, yes.' She sighed. 'I know I'm just a foolish old woman but I still have dreams, dreams that one day— '

She was interrupted by a knock on the door.

'Come in,' she called out sharply.

The maid entered carrying a bouquet of red and white carnations. 'These have just arrived for you, ma'am,' she said.

To Samson's astonishment Mrs Huntingdon-Winstanley keeled forward in her chair and flopped on to the table apparently in a dead faint.

Chapter 6

'Quick, get a glass of water,' said Samson and the maid still holding the bunch of carnations, sped from the room.

Fearing the old woman had succumbed to a heart attack Samson eased her upright. He was glad to hear her breathing but her eyes were still closed. She was wearing a peculiarly pungent perfume which caught at his nostrils as he gently straightened a wig which had been knocked askew when she'd lurched forward on to the table. He was surprised that her hair hadn't been her own. The wig was a perfectly constructed deception and it was obvious why she wore it. The part of her scalp which had been revealed was thinly covered with wispy white hair.

The maid returned carrying a glass of water on a silver salver.

'You'd better call her doctor,' said Samson.

Eyes behind black-rimmed spectacles widened with alarm. 'I can't do that, sir. Madam won't have doctors. She believes in herbs and the like, what they call medicine of the alternative sort.'

Mrs Huntingdon-Winstanley opened her eyes. 'No doctors,' she whispered, 'and take those flowers away, Jennifer.'

'I already have, madam. Are you all right?'

'Quite all right, thank you. Now go.'

As the maid began to move away she was peremptorily halted.

'Just a minute. Who sent the flowers?'

'I don't know, madam.'

'What do you mean, you don't know? There must have been a note.'

She spoke with an acerbity which showed she had recovered from the faint.

'There wasn't a note, madam.'

'Then who delivered the flowers?'

'I don't know. A man.'

'What man? And how did he get into the building?'

'The hall 'phoned to say there was a delivery man with flowers and could he be sent up. I said yes.'

'I didn't know about this. Why wasn't I told?'

The maid hung her head. 'I didn't want to disturb you. I knew you had this gentleman with you.'

'In future do disturb me. I don't like strangers to come up here. Now go.'

The maid scuttled from the room. As the door closed Mrs Huntingdon-Winstanley turned to Samson and, after taking a sip of water, said, 'It's so difficult to get good staff these days. Perhaps you've noticed it yourself. The agency sent me Jennifer. She's only been with me a month and hasn't learned my ways. I'm not a difficult woman and yet I do seem to have difficulty in getting and keeping suitable staff.' She took another sip of water. 'But never mind about that. I'm sorry about my temporary indisposition. A moment of weakness.'

'You were upset by the sight of the flowers?'

She paused before replying. 'Well, yes. I'm very superstitious. Some nurses are, you know. We would never allow a bunch of red and white flowers to be brought into the ward when I was with the NHS. It means a death in the ward. . . . I'm feeling better now. I wonder who could have sent them.'

'Possibly someone who knows of the superstition.'

'Yes . . . possibly . . .' She took a deep breath. 'I've recovered my composure,' she said. 'What were we talking about?'

81

'Your will.'

'Oh, yes. I'm not going to discuss that further so please don't talk about it.'

Samson resumed his seat on the far side of the table.

'Has your husband always collected books?' he asked. 'When did he start collecting?'

'When? Let me think. I'm not so good on recent dates. It's odd how one remembers the distant past so clearly but not the immediate past.'

'So it's a fairly recent hobby?'

'Oh, yes. Within the last five years.'

'Did he visit France frequently before then?'

'No. We went everywhere together and I preferred Greece or America for holidays. It's really only since I had this wretched arthritis, and we took on Robert, that he's been visiting France so often although I must say he's always been interested in French literature. But not seriously. Not old books.'

'Have you ever met this surgeon friend of your husband's?' Samson asked.

The question seemed to disconcert her and for a moment he was afraid she was about to have another fainting attack. But she took a sip of water and recovered her poise.

'Of course I haven't met him,' she said. 'I didn't even know he was a surgeon, did I? I thought he must be a dealer in rare books. Until Simon telephoned from that place – what's its name? – I didn't even know he had a friend there.'

A silence fell. It occurred to Samson that the oppressively warm room might have contributed to his client's faint. 'Do you ever go out for fresh air?' he asked.

'No. I'm housebound. I don't want to go out, anyway. It's a different world from the one I once knew. I see it on television and read about it in newspapers and want nothing of it.'

Samson picked up his briefcase and placed it on his

ample lap. 'I'm not sure there's much more I can do at the moment,' he said. 'We'll have to wait until your husband returns to this country.' He stood up. 'Is there anything you want to ask before I go?'

'No, I don't think so. Thank you for coming, even if it was inconveniently late and has caused me to miss the latest episode of *Coronation Street*. And if you see that girl on your way out tell her to get rid of the flowers, will you?'

'I will.'

Night had fallen by the time he left the apartment block. As he passed through the reception area he smiled to a new security guard who gave him a baleful look in return. He took a taxi back to his own flat. It had been a long day and he was tired.

He mixed a long glass of gin and tonic with ice and a thick slice of lime before cooking a meal of chicken in white wine sauce with ratatouille and sauté potatoes. He followed this with chocolate profiteroles which had been purchased for him from Marks and Spencer by his twice-a-week housekeeper, Mrs Collas. To hell with calories, he thought. Hunger satisfied, he had a Benedictine and coffee before retiring to bed.

He was falling asleep when the telephone rang. He switched on a bedside lamp and picked up the handset.

'Samson here.'

'I'm sorry to be calling you so late, Mr Samson, but I've just remembered something.'

It was Mrs Huntingdon-Winstanley.

'Think nothing of it,' he said. 'I caused you to miss an episode of *Coronation Street*; you're entitled to cause me to lose some sleep.'

'Ha! Very good. *Touché*. One up to you. No, I've just remembered the name of that man. The killer from Spain. It wasn't Biggs or Buck, or whatever I said. It was Hawkey. Two syllables, not one. Isn't it odd how one's memory plays one false?'

'Hawkey. I'll make a note of it,' said Samson wearily. 'Good night.'

The following morning he arrived at his office to find that Shandy had put vases of flowers around the place. They had the effect of both brightening the office and emphasising its desolation. Shandy had also acquired three chairs. 'We can't expect clients to stand,' she said.

'I'm glad the flowers aren't a mix of red and white,' he replied, and went on to tell her of the interview with Mrs Huntingdon-Winstanley on the previous evening.

'Superstitious old bird,' Shandy commented. 'So what's your next move?'

'Have I got any appointments today?'

'Only one this morning. Mrs Cumbermack.'

'Give her a call and fix something for tomorrow. Explain that the office isn't what it should be but all her papers are intact. I'm going to see a Mrs Brightwell.'

'You've found out where Brightwell lived?'

'I knew he didn't belong to the Association of Private Investigators, and he wasn't in the Yellow Pages, so before I came here I began calling all the Brightwells in the telephone directory.'

'Doing my job,' she interrupted.

He smiled. 'I thought I'd leave you to get on with slum clearance. Anyway, it didn't take long. I struck lucky with the fifth call. I explained that I was a p. i. and was trying to trace a fellow p. i. who probably had information which would help on one of my cases. I'd be willing to pay for any information, and pay generously.'

'You must have been speaking to his widow,' said Shandy.

'That's right. She explained that her husband had been killed in a motor accident. I asked whether she knew where his papers might be and if his practice had been sold. She said it wasn't a practice as such. He operated from home and she had been his secretary. She thought she might be able to help me, and asked what was the information I needed. Whom did it concern? When I said it was Mrs H-W a change came over her. At first she pretended not to remember the name and I had to press hard to get her to agree to see me, said I'd pay even if when she went through her husband's papers she couldn't find anything relevant. In other words, I'd pay for nothing, but I'd like to see her. She asked what sort of sum I was offering and I said fifty for no information but two hundred for good information.

'And she bought it?'

'Yes. I got the impression she might be quite hard up.' He looked at his watch. 'I'd better be going.'

Mrs Brightwell lived in a small terrace house in a back street of the London borough of Haringey. Because the houses had been built for working-class occupation long before that class became part of a car-owning democracy there were no garages and this accounted for the cars and vans parked bumper to bumper on both sides of the street. Some of the houses had perished paintwork on doors and window frames, and brickwork which needed repointing; others showed a pride in ownership and were like soldiers on a parade which had oddly been infiltrated by a few tramps. Samson was pleased to observe that number 57, where Mrs Brightwell lived, had its doorstep gleaming with red cardinal polish and its windows shielded by fresh white net curtains.

He pressed a bell and heard chimes from within. The front door was opened by a woman whose mousey brown hair was worn in a fringe above big brown eyes. She was wearing a smock and was obviously pregnant. Two children aged about six and five clung to the dress. 'Mr Samson?' she asked.

'I am.'

She invited him inside and said to the children, 'Now

you go and watch the telly while Mum talks with this gentleman.' To Samson she said, 'We'll go into the front room.'

She cleared a bale of curtain material from a chair and said, 'Would you like to sit down, Mr Samson?'

The room looked like a workshop. In addition to curtain materials there was a row of men's and women's clothes hanging on a rail. The room was dominated by a table supporting an electric sewing machine.

'I was doing this even when Reg was alive,' she explained, 'making curtains and doing tailoring alterations. I had to. He was unemployed, you see.'

'Not a private investigator?'

She gave a sad smile. 'He called himself that but the place didn't exactly hum with business. What there was was mostly debt collecting and a bit of process serving. It wasn't easy after he left the Force.'

'He was a policeman?'

She nodded.

'May I ask, why did he leave?'

She flinched slightly. 'The whole thing was a fix. A frame up. He was the scapegoat. Someone had to go. It was a death in custody but he didn't touch the fellow.' A tired look came to her eyes. 'He was very bitter about it and got very depressed. But after a while he pulled himself together and started trying to set himself up as a private detective. He reckoned he'd had enough experience in that line, you see.'

Samson did see. A number of ex-policemen went into the business of private investigation. What he didn't understand was how a novice private eye should get a client like Mrs Huntingdon-Winstanley, and he asked this.

'It was funny really,' she replied. 'We'd had a handbill from a window-cleaner pushed through the letter-box. Reg looked at it and said, "I think I'll have some like this printed off for me, advertising myself." I laughed. I said, "Where are you going to distribute them? You won't get any custom around here." "I'm thinking of circulating them in some posh up-market area," he said, "by mail possibly. I can get names and addresses off the electoral register." I must say, Mr Samson, I thought it was a waste of time and money, but he did get one response. Mrs Huntingdon-Winstanley.'

She went across the room to a small bureau and took out a slim sheaf of papers in a manila folder.

'You said you'd pay for information.'

'That's right.' Samson took out his wallet and extracted sixty pounds and laid the notes next to the sewing machine. 'That's just for allowing me to visit you. There's another hundred and forty if you'll let me glance through those papers.'

Her expressive brown eyes were filled with uncertainty. 'I didn't know you actually wanted to read them. They're confidential notes.'

'I appreciate that, but how did you expect to deliver the goods if I'm not to see your husband's notes?'

'I thought you'd ask questions and I'd try to find the answers in the notes.'

Samson slowly shook his head. It looked as measured and emphatic as a hippopotamus might appear if trying to clear its head of a hangover.

'Oh, all right then,' Mrs Brightwell sighed. 'Here you are.'

Before taking the papers Samson laid the balance of money on the sewing table.

'Thank you. Much obliged, I'm sure. If you don't mind I'll finish a dress alteration. It's needed for tonight. A party at the Assembly Rooms. I hope it won't disturb you.'

'It won't. Not a bit.'

For the next half hour he read and made notes while the sewing machine hummed.

Mrs Huntingdon-Winstanley had asked Brightwell to find out what he could about Robert Mansour. She'd said she suspected him of being a con man out to fleece her husband. She wanted him followed wherever he went.

Samson reflected that his predecessor had received a different brief and wondered why his client had decided to give him instructions which focused on her husband rather than the manservant. He also wondered if Mrs Huntingdon-Winstanley had lured Brightwell into playing spillikins. There was no reference to the game in the notes. Perhaps Brightwell hadn't passed the delicacy-of-touch test.

Reading through the notes it was clear Brightwell had made enquiries of various government agencies and information bureaux. He had also, through a contact he had retained in the police force, discovered that Robert Mansour had no criminal record and that he possessed dual nationality.

Some papers held together by a paper clip were more interesting. Brightwell had obtained copies of the references given by Robert when he applied for the post of chauffeur-valet. One was on House of Commons notepaper and the other from a peer of the realm. Both letters spoke of Robert Mansour as conscientious and trustworthy, and excellent at his job. These were unexceptional references but what intrigued Samson was Brightwell's written comment.

Contacted referees. Both refused to comment. Lord P very snotty and threatened to have me thrown off the premises and would set his solicitor on me if I troubled him again. MP more subtle. Claimed he couldn't spare time to discuss such matters which were strictly confidential anyway. Polite but nervous. Well he might be. Probably thought I was investigating *him*. He once nearly got done for cottaging. Lord P has same inclinations; both get their jollies the gay way. Where did they come across RM? Is he ex rent-boy? Is there some secret gay club? Could SW be one of those? Maybe it isn't con job at all. Would client be pleased to know the truth if the truth is coloured gay?

The last item held by the clip was a note in pencil written below a cutting from the *Daily Mail* gossip column which had been pasted to a piece of paper. The columnist reported that 'A certain English aristocrat is again cruising the Mediterranean in his yacht and will no doubt call at Alexandria, a favoured watering-hole. Expect to see his yacht there surrounded by buoys. Me lord likes privacy.'

Underneath the cutting Brightwell had written, 'Very neat. I like the reference to cruising and buoys. Bet Lord P won't dare to get his solicitor on to that. He'll have to grin and bear it.'

The next item in the sheaf of papers was an unmounted cutting from a glossy men's magazine. It was headed, 'Cosmetic Surgery for Men' and offered procedures for nose improvement, correction to bat ears and receding chin, the elimination of turkey-gobble throat, and treatment for baldness. The advertisement had been inserted by an organisation called the Piccadilly Clinic. The clinic's address was nowhere near Piccadilly being at Mill Hill in north London. The telephone number of the clinic had been heavily ringed in blue ballpoint ink. Attached to the cutting was a note in Brightwell's hand. 'Taken from a magazine junked into a litter bin by RM after leaving Indian restaurant in Baker Street. Had seen him buy magazine earlier from bookstall near underground station. Why interested in this clinic?'

Samson paused from reading. There was a possible link between a surgeon resident in Nonancourt and a clinic in north London, but why should Robert and Winstanley – whom Shandy had dubbed 'the dynamic duo' after the cartoon characters Robin and Batman – why should they be

89

interested in cosmetic surgery? The clinic's services related to men, not women, and if Mrs Huntingdon-Winstanley hoped her husband's concern with surgery was to benefit her it was a hope unlikely to be realised. Samson wished he had studied Winstanley's face more closely and looked for evidence of surgery.

He put down the magazine cutting and continued persuing Brightwell's records. Some papers from a different investigation involving a stolen dog had become mixed up with them and he spent a couple of minutes extracting these. The next relevant paper was a letter from the embassy of the United Arab Emirates politely disclaiming knowledge of one Robert Mansour and suggesting that any further enquiry be addressed to the Bureau of Internal Affairs in Cairo.

And then Samson found a couple of pages torn from a notebook in which Brightwell had written in pencil about his sighting of Hawkey with Winstanley and Robert Mansour.

Tailed them to Hyde Park. RM got out leaving boss in car. Met man by Albert Mem. Back to car. Not able to see man clearly but something familiar about him. Stayed well away to avoid suspicion. After thirteen minutes man got out of car and RM and SW drove off. Decided not to follow RM but to concentrate on man. Was right. Had seen him before. Seven years ago in West End nick. Known for GBH offences and suspected of two contract killings but not proved. Involved in security van hold-up when guard was killed, not by him. Grassed on the others and got only five years. Got nickname 'Squwarky' Hawkey and last heard of living under different name in Spain. Why he come back here? Must advise client to have extreme care for her safety. RM may be after her money. May have conned boss into some project needing financial backing (e.g. cosmetic clinics for men) and suggesting that if Mrs H-W out of way, and SW inherits, he could make good profits by backing venture. Maybe would even try to get boss to do the dirty after she's gone to bed for the night. More likely to enlist Hawkey.

After he had copied the note Samson studied the final paper in the sheaf. It was another page torn from a notebook.

7 Feb. 11.35 a.m. Client 'phones to say she's overheard SW arranging to go to Isle of Wight tomorrow. Going by car, Portsmouth to Fishbourne ferry. Why they go to IOW? What there in Feb? (Memories of honeymoon with Jackie at Ventnor. What a farce!) But why IOW? Visiting a prisoner in Parkhurst jail? Is that the tie-up with Hawkey? He wants RM to get message through to someone there? An escape plan?

Samson put the sheaf of papers back in the manila folder. Mrs Brightwell looked up from sewing a hem and saw he had finished reading. After stopping the machine she asked, 'Have you finished, Mr Samson?'

'Yes, thanks. Just one or two questions, if I may.'

'Yes?' It sounded an apprehensive affirmative.

'I'm sorry to bring up unhappy memories but what was the date of your husband's accident?'

'It's all right. The eighth of February, actually.'

'May I ask your first name?'

'Carol. Why?'

'Was your husband married previously?'

'Yes.' She hesitated. 'I don't know what it's got to do with the price of tea but he was married to someone who was already pregnant by another man. He got the marriage annulled. I met him a few months later and we fell in love.' Her hand went instinctively to her bulging abdomen and tears came to her eyes. 'He was a good man and a good

91

father. We loved each other. He was so proud when I fell again. Said it was the best incentive he could have for making a success of his new job.'

'Did he ever mention the name Hawkey to you?'

'Oh, yes. I heard about him.'

'Did he give any opinion why Hawkey might have come back to England from Spain?'

'Yes. Hawkey knew he'd be marked for grassing and although he was a hard man himself he was afraid another hard man would be sent out to get him and he had a plan to spring someone from Parkhurst. It would be a sort of penance to take the heat off himself. Or that's what Reg thought. And he reckoned the man called RM might have ways and means, or his boss might.'

'Did Reg ever talk about cosmetic surgery?'

'Cosmetic surgery? No. Why?'

'I just wondered. You were his secretary. He might have mentioned something.'

She gave a nervous laugh. 'Secretary! I was called that for the sake of appearances. So he could talk about his secretary and claim a tax allowance. The reality was that I did all this' – she waved her hand at the row of clothes – 'someone had to make the money.'

'What was the coroner's verdict on Reg's death?'

'Accidental,' she replied with unexpected force. 'Unbelievable, isn't it? He'd had his car serviced the day before by some cowboy on the cheap. Reg had complained about the brakes and I reckon this cowboy, who didn't really know what he was doing, did something which made the braking more dangerous than it already was, but my lawyer said nothing could be proved. No negligence. So that was that.'

'I think that's all,' said Samson, standing up. 'If anything else occurs to me I'll get in touch. I may be in touch anyway.' He patted his waistline. 'I'm being badgered into losing a bit of weight. Some of my clothes may need alteration.'

She opened a drawer and took out a card. 'Here's my card, Mr Samson. Alterations within twenty-four hours. My terms are very reasonable. I'd be glad to assist.' She rose rather awkwardly to her feet. 'I'll see you out and find out what those little devils have been up to. You can't trust them out of your sight for a minute, I can tell you.'

Samson followed her out of the room. As she approached the front door she turned and asked, 'Have you got any children of your own, Mr Samson?'

'No.'

'Oh, I'm sorry.'

'Yes, not to have children is a great misfortune,' said Samson, but the serious tone of his voice belied his true feelings. From experience he regarded children as a pain rather than a pleasure although in dark moments, when lying awake at three in the morning and wondering what was the point of life, if there was any point at all, he sometimes wished he had been married and blessed not only with a child but grandchildren also.

Chapter 7

Although Samson didn't regard himself as a lucky man, by a stroke of good fortune office premises on the third floor of a building in King Street, close to his new flat, were on the market. The premium was exorbitant and the lease had a mere nine years to run at a high rent but the place was more spacious than his present fire-damaged office and needed little in the way of alteration to make it suitable for the purpose of his agency. He took Shandy to view the premises.

'I like it,' she said. 'I'll have space to move around and not be obliged to work with nervous clients waiting in the same room as me. It has a separate waiting room *and* its own loo. What luxury! I'm all in favour.'

'I'll go and see the vendor's agents, and my solicitor, and make sure speed is of the essence. You get back to base and hold the fort. I'll join you later.'

It was late in the afternoon when he rejoined her. She was sitting by her word-processor painting her finger-nails.

'The police have been in touch,' she said. 'They are reasonably sure the fire was started by some vandal of the well-known mindless variety. Apparently there's an amateur arsonist around and a man answering to the description given by the Kirmani child has been sighted at the time and places of the fires. It must have been coincidence that this chap could have resembled the fellow who tried to do you that night.'

'I wonder if any statistician has ever worked out how

many incidences there must be before a coincidence comes along,' said Samson throwing his raincoat over a chair, 'or if anyone has ever formulated a law of coincidence. If so, I'd be interested to hear about it.'

Shandy rolled her eyes to a smoke-blackened ceiling indicating more clearly than words that interest wasn't mutual.

'I believe there's a Hindu saying,' he went on, 'that if traced far enough back all coincidence becomes inevitable.'

'Fascinating.'

'Speaking of coincidence,' he continued, 'it may be a coincidence that Brightwell found an advertisement for a cosmetic clinic in England, and Winstanley and Mansour visited a cosmetic surgeon in France. The two facts might just be a coincidence, neither having any bearing on the other.'

Shandy screwed on the cap of a bottle of nail varnish. 'That's my cosmetics done for the day,' she said, 'unless Paul takes me out for a meal tonight.'

Samson wasn't listening. Preoccupied by a train of thought he was slowly pacing up and down the room.

'If the dynamic duo have some real interest in cosmetic surgery, and they have an assignation with a known villain, it isn't too far-fetched to wonder if said villain wants his features rearranged and the dynamic duo are go-betweens.' He stopped pacing and faced Shandy. 'Or is it just a coincidence that two men apparently involved in the world of cosmetic surgery should meet someone who might need such a service to conceal his identity?'

'I don't know.' She waved her hands to dry the nail varnish. 'You're the detective. I'm just an acolyte, floozie and paid hanger-on.'

'Is it just coincidence,' he went on, 'that Brightwell who was working for Mrs H-W was killed in a car which had brake failure and I, now working for her, could have been killed in the same way?'

Shandy remained silent and Samson answered his own question. 'I don't think it was a coincidence but I don't understand what there is in a cosmetic surgery set-up to warrant homicide. There's something more to it. Well, we'll have to wait and see. Until I get another summons from Mrs H-W the case can rest.'

Shandy examined her finger-nails. 'I don't know about the law of coincidences,' she said, 'but I can tell you about another law, Sod's Law.'

'The law that things going wrong will happen at the most inconvenient time?'

'Right. Just when we could do with a lull in business we're overworked. When I got in, the answerphone was packed with messages, people wanting urgent appointments. And I've got any number of calls to make after I've had a word with you.'

Samson shook his head sadly. 'You are the picture of an overworked secretary.'

She held up her hands. 'These?' she asked. 'It's the best thing to do, or something like this, if you're under pressure. Take a break. Let the mind go blank.'

'Well, you can unblank your mind. What's on?'

When she had finished reading a list he said, 'The sooner we move office, the better. I've got a completion date and so you can start making a list of people who should receive change of address notification. I want all clients to be informed. . . .'

'Every client we've ever had?' she exclaimed.

'Every client within the last two or three years, and all contacts who have been useful as well as regulars like Bernard and Anton.'

'The other day you said something about a rise. Was that just promises, promises?'

'It was for real, and what's more you're going to get

an assistant, somebody to do the dogsbody jobs. The extra room can serve as a place for filing cabinets and a waiting room. We'll have a small telephone switchboard there operated by someone who doubles as a copy typist and receptionist.'

Shandy regarded him quizzically. 'This sounds like some sort of promotion for me.'

'Yes.'

She stood up.

'Where are you going?' he asked.

She picked up the bottle of nail varnish labelled 'Quiet pink'. I'm just going to put this in the fridge and then it's all systems 'Go'.

In the hectic days of trying to keep a business operating smoothly during a period of changing offices Samson would have been glad, if he'd thought about it, that Mrs Huntingdon-Winstanley didn't contact him. In this respect, at least, Sod's Law was in abeyance.

It was the second day after the move to King Street that the case presented itself again but not through his client. He was in the middle of interviewing a young woman to be Shandy's assistant (Shandy had already seen her and approved) when Shandy put through a call.

'Sorry to interrupt you, but it's Mrs Brightwell and she sounds very upset. Can you take the call?'

'Put her through.'

A distraught voice came thinly down the line. 'Mr Samson, something terrible has happened. I've been burgled!'

Samson's response was immediate and practical. 'Then you must notify the police. It's a criminal matter.'

'I don't think you understand. I've been burgled but nothing was stolen.'

Samson's interest quickened. 'Tell me about it.'

'Someone must have broken in during the night while

we were all asleep. When I came down this morning I found Reg's bureau had been broken into and all his papers and documents were scattered around. Nothing was taken so far as I can tell. I can't go to the police on a thing like that, but it's worried me stiff.'

'It seems as though someone was looking for certain documents and not concerned with anything else. You say there's nothing missing – what about the papers you let me see?'

'I got rid of them after you left.'

'Why did you do that?'

There was a slight pause and then, her voice more controlled, Mrs Brightwell said, 'After you left, I thought about it. I knew Reg thought the case could be risky, dangerous. It wasn't like any of the others which were all tame stuff. I decided I didn't want to keep the papers. It sounds silly, but I didn't want to be reminded any more. I mean, it was while he was working on that case that Reg died. It was a bad luck thing.'

'How did you get rid of the papers?'

'I took them into the back yard and burned them and I put the ashes in the dustbin.'

'How many people knew that you kept Reg's papers in that bureau?'

'I can't say. Quite a few I should think.'

'And how many knew about my visit?'

Her reply was quick and assured. 'Nobody. I kept that quiet. To be honest, I felt a bit bad. I mean, taking all that money for something private. I wouldn't want anyone to know I'd been selling private information.'

'I don't think your burglar will return, Mrs Brightwell. He may have been searching for papers relating to the case I've taken over, found nothing, and probably he'll assume there's nothing to be found. But if you have any more trouble in that direction, get in touch with me again.'

'I don't need to go to the police, do I?'

'Not if you don't want to.'

'Thank you, Mr Samson. Goodbye.'

Samson put down the handset and turned to his interviewee, a young woman who had high cheekbones, a pert nose and a small chin. She was wearing a trim dark blue two-piece and looked like the archetypal office girl.

'The first time I ever saw you,' said Samson, 'was in a pub frequented by punks and yuppies. Do you remember?'

The young woman winced. 'Don't remind me.'

'Your hair was a pink bush striped with orange; you had a ring on every finger of both hands and wore skintight black leather pants,' Samson pursued remorselessly.

'I've changed. Look.' She ruffled soft brown hair with ringless fingers. 'And I don't wear punk gear any more although I'm not really into outfits like this one.'

'I'll draw a veil over what you were doing the next time I saw you.'

'I wish you would, Mr Samson.'

He had rescued her from the attentions of four youths and paid for a mini-cab to take her home.*

'I know you applied for a job once before,' he said, 'but we weren't quite ready for a third member of the firm. However, I did promise to keep you in mind and Shandy is willing to give you a trial run. Has she told you what you'd have to do?'

Samson's heavily lidded eyes had become like two alert creatures which had emerged from their burrows. The young woman's eyes matched his for brightness. 'Yes, I've been told.' She sat forward eagerly.

Samson stood up and extended his hand. 'Welcome to the firm, Georgia. Shandy will tell you when to start and fill you in on all details. You know the salary. It's not negotiable and I don't pay overtime.'

*The incident appears in detail in *One Lover Too Many*.

99

'I don't care. It's a decent job.'

'And goodbye to – all that?'

Her pretty face clouded. 'You bet,' she said. 'Punters can punt off.'

For a few moments after she left the room Samson indulged in reminiscence. He had been very surprised when the girl he had rescued from an invited fate had turned up at his office to repay the price of a mini-cab fare. She had stayed for a cup of tea and Shandy had liked her, but from that time until now, there had been silence. With the passage of time she had improved both image and grammar, and Samson was glad to give her a chance. As someone who had never known a father, and come up the hard way, he felt sympathy for the underprivileged even though he knew that the underprivileged could be no less greedy, opportunistic and self-seeking than the privileged.

His reverie was broken by Shandy's voice on the intercom. 'It's Mrs H-W on the 'phone for you,' she said.

'Put her through.'

Mrs Huntingdon-Winstanley's voice was so loud that Samson held the handset about two inches from his right ear.

'Mr Samson. Disaster. They've stolen a march on me. They've gone again but I wasn't told until the moment they were leaving. It was too late to inform you. I don't know what ...' Her voice trailed away. Samson pressed the handset to his ear and could just hear breathing. And then, 'I'm sorry, you'll have to excuse me. I'm not feeling too well. Could you call me back in about half an hour?' Without waiting for a reply she rang off.

Samson replaced the handset. A dormant case had been resurrected twice within an hour, first by Mrs Brightwell and now by Mrs Huntingdon-Winstanley. Surely this was an example of coincidence; nothing sinister or supernatural could be read into it, and yet he felt there was some elusive connection between apparently dissimilar and unrelated events.

His heavy head retracted into his shoulders like a tortoise head retracting into its carapace as he sunk himself in thought.

The case had begun with a summons to Mrs Huntingdon-Winstanley's apartment. Here there had been some bizarre game-playing before he'd been engaged to find evidence that her husband was, with a manservant's connivance, having a series of affairs with women, and she had wanted to know what the two men were up to. She had purported to be someone having a controlling interest in a large company which manufactured costume jewellery.

Somehow her husband had got wind of the assignment and called at his, Samson's, office. This had been followed by an attack in an alleyway one night and then his office had been damaged in an arson attempt. In France he had tracked his quarry not realising that his pursuit was known. Odd events in a small hotel where he had suddenly become *persona non grata* had been followed by discovering a man tampering with his car's braking system. Then he had been knocked out by an unseen, but not unsmelled, assailant.

Were all or some of the incidents inter-related, and was Winstanley behind them, or was some third party involved?'

At his next meeting with Mrs Huntingdon-Winstanley she had revealed that her wealth was inherited from her husband's father because she had faithfully nursed the old man. But such a bequest could have led to resentment on Winstanley's part. He would feel that the dead man's estate should rightfully be his.

And against this complex background, yet somehow to be merged into the overall picture, was the fact that Winstanley was friendly with a cosmetic surgeon and that cosmetic surgery might well be a factor in the case if Brightwell's findings were added to his own.

Mrs Huntingdon-Winstanley had said she was afraid her husband was mixed up with some illegal activity. Was this activity connected both with convicted criminals and cosmetics?

His train of thought was interrupted by Shandy on the intercom.

'Georgia would like to start next Monday. Is that okay?'

'Fine. You've briefed her on all her duties?'

'Of course.'

'Including my comestible requirements?'

'Your calorie-controlled snacks, yes.'

'Next Monday then.' Samson glanced at his watch. 'And would you get me Mrs H-W in five minutes' time.'

It was difficult to resume his train of thought. In some cases, and this was such an instance, he was like a variety artist who throws a number of skittles into the air and juggles with them. One skittle he hadn't yet incorporated into the act had 'homosexual circle' written on its side. The gathering at the house by the bridge had appeared from laughter overheard to be exclusively male. Mrs Huntingdon-Winstanley had hinted that her husband was bisexual. Brightwell had discovered that Robert Mansour's referees were men who were homosexually orientated and Brightwell had, in his notes, written of Mansour, 'Is he ex rent-boy? Is there some secret gay club?'

Samson was no nearer to finding a common denominator between the various factors in the case when Shandy informed him that she had obtained his call.

'I hope you're feeling better, Mrs Huntingdon-Winstanley.'

'Much better, thank you. I get these indispositions. Unfortunately they are becoming more frequent but don't tell me to consult a doctor. Some are all right but most are a lot of quacks who dish out pills recommended by drug companies who have lavishly wined and dined them. I've worked in the medical profession, I

102

know. No, I believe in Nature's remedies. But enough of that. As I was telling you, the birds have flown the nest and I don't see what can be done now. I shall just have to do without knowing what my husband is up to. It's a worry I'll have to put up with. You don't have any suggestions, I suppose?'

'How many staff do you have?' Samson asked.

'Staff? Well, there's Jennifer, my maid. And Robert, of course. And then there's a woman who comes in to do general domestic duties.'

'No cook?' Samson enquired.

'No. I like to see to my own food. I don't eat a lot and am mainly vegetarian. This doesn't suit Simon who has what is known as a hearty appetite. He's a trencherman. But he enjoys cooking and so does Robert. If they don't eat out they cook for themselves. Why do you ask?'

'Does Jennifer have any time off?'

'Naturally she does. Every Wednesday afternoon and every other week-end, plus a fortnight's annual holiday when she's been with me a year.'

'And how do you manage personally in her absence?'

'The agency can sometimes supply a temporary maid. I have to pay the earth, of course, and usually get some incompetent. Recently I've done my best to manage on my own. But I don't see the point of all these questions.'

'The point,' said Samson, 'is that I'd like to come and see you on a day when nobody else is around.'

'Just the two of us, you mean?'

'Just the two of us.'

'I'm not sure . . . I don't wish to be compromised . . .'

A silence fell. Who, Samson wondered, could possibly suspect anyone of wanting to have an illicit affair with Mrs Huntingdon-Winstanley? Who would contemplate kissing those thin scarlet-waxed lips or those encrusted flame-red cheeks?

The silence was broken by her voice. 'All right then. But you mustn't tell anyone. I don't want anyone to know a man is visiting me while I'm on my own.'

'And you mustn't tell anyone, either.'

'Mr Samson! The very thought that I would! Certainly not. But wait a minute. The doorman on the ground floor will know. Nobody gets past him.'

'Don't worry about that,' said Samson. 'I've had a good look at the building and there's a fire escape at the back which can be reached by going through a tradesman's entrance. If you can manage to release the door handle at the top of the escape I can enter and leave that way.'

'You might be seen going up.'

'There's only one point in the street from which I could be seen and I'll arrange it that I'm not observed.'

'How can you do that?'

'I can. Take my word for it. All you have to do is to make sure I can get in.'

'Very well. I must say it's been encouraging to speak to you. I'd thought all was lost.'

'What day will you be completely free?' Samson asked.

'Wednesday. Next Wednesday afternoon and evening.'

'Have the fire-escape door open by two o'clock in the afternoon provided the coast is clear at your end.'

'Ha! This is rather fun, isn't it? It reminds me of when I was a girl. I went to boarding school. Pranks in the dorm, you know.'

Samson didn't know about girlish pranks, but what he did know was that the time had come to end the conversation.

'Good day, Mrs Huntingdon-Winstanley. I'll look forward to seeing you next Wednesday afternoon at two.'

Why, he wondered, as he replaced the handset, did he get a sort of amused pleasure out of pronouncing her double-barrelled name, giving each of the six syllables due weight. Later, he put this question to Shandy.

'It's the pleasure of harmless mockery,' she said. 'Underneath it all, you must quite like Mrs H-W.'

Samson laughed. 'What makes you say that?'

Shandy didn't echo his laugh. She was serious when she said, 'We only exercise harmless mockery on those we care about; on others it's malicious mockery, or we don't bother.'

Chapter 8

'The best way to lose a tail,' Samson informed Georgia, 'isn't, as you might think, by driving fast in a car. It's by exploiting the advantages of London's underground train system.'

'Is that what we're doing then?' she asked as they hurried down the Green Park escalator. 'Losing a tail?'

'I don't know whether we're being followed, but if we are, we shall lose him.'

'Or her.'

'Or her,' repeated Samson giving his companion a side-long glance while wondering if he'd acquired an active feminist.

From King's Cross station Samson took a taxi to Regent's Park. Outside Mrs Huntingdon-Winstanley's apartment block he said, 'You see that fire escape?'

'Yes.'

'It's only visible for about ten yards of each side of where we're standing. I want you to stay here while I go up it. If you see any pedestrian in the vicinity before I start climbing I don't want you to do anything but if there's no one likely to be in this area for twenty seconds or so I want you to shift the strap of your shoulder bag from one shoulder to the other. That'll be the signal for me to go. Understood?'

'Yes. But what then?'

'You'll have to keep watch for when I appear at the top of the fire escape. It might be quite a long wait.

When I do appear, if the coast is clear for me to come down, shift your bag around. If not, do nothing and I'll wait until you give the signal.' He gave her a close look. 'Okay?'

She smiled. 'I'll say it's okay. I've only been with you two days and here I am on a case. It's great.'

'It'll be less great when you've been here for a couple of hours and it's started raining.'

She shrugged. 'I don't care. I've got a plastic mack and hood. Not that I like wearing naff gear but you did tell me to have it handy.'

Cars were passing as they stood on the pavement. They were an oddly matched couple; a big middle-aged man in Burberry raincoat holding a large black bag beside a petite young woman wearing trainers, old blue jeans and a roll-neck blue-green sweater.

'Right,' he said. 'I'm on my way.'

'Don't be too long. I don't want to attract the attention of punters.'

'You can cope with that, can't you?'

She smiled broadly. 'Of course I can. I know how to say "Piss Off" in seventeen different languages.'

'Good. See you later.'

Gripping the bag which contained his necessary equipment Samson moved through a side gate marked 'Tradesman's Entrance' and made for the foot of the fire escape.

Mrs Huntingdon-Winstanley was waiting for him. Her apparel was strikingly different from Georgia's. She was wearing an evening dress of hyacinth blue satin with leg-of-mutton sleeves. Pearl drop earrings hung from her ears matching a one-string necklace having pearls of equal size. Samson had the uneasy suspicion that she had dressed to kill and he was the intended victim.

'Isn't this exciting!' she exclaimed.

'Very,' he replied drily, edging away from her.

'Now you're here, do you feel like a game of Spillikins?

107

I'm so ashamed of the performance I put up last time. I'm sure I'll be better today.'

'No games,' said Samson firmly. 'I've got work to do. There's nobody here, I hope?'

'Nobody at all. We're alone together.'

'Good. I'll start with the sitting room. I want to go through your husband's entire collection of books.'

She looked startled. 'There's quite a lot. You aren't going to attempt to read them?'

'No. But you could save me time if you could tell me the names of the towns he usually visits when he's looking for purchases.'

She began hobbling, right foot drooping, towards the sitting room.

'I can't do that. He never tells me. I'm not really interested. Those times I have asked where he's been I get some vague reply like "Paris" or "here and there".' She turned towards him. 'Why do you want to know?'

Samson never disclosed reasons for his actions unless necessary. 'I like to be methodical,' he replied with a smile.

'Ha!'

While he went through books in the sitting room she shuffled a pack of cards and played games of patience.

His motive for examining the books was simple. Dealers in second-hand books would sometimes affix a small adhesive label inside the cover which gave their name and address. Samson opened more than two hundred books and found eleven with such labels. Three were from Orléans, two from Amboise, one from Blois and three from Azay-le-Rideau.

The search took him less than half an hour. He paused before replacing the last of the marked books, a second edition of the posthumously published *Histoire du romantisme* by Théophile Gautier. This book which had been purchased at Azay-le-Rideau added weight to a theory he had begun to formulate. All towns were associated with the valley of the river Loire; all were in what was known as 'château country'. Winstanley hadn't scoured the length of France for his books but seemed to have concentrated on one area. And Nonancourt was on the direct route from Boulogne to château country. Whatever reason Winstanley had for visiting France, apart from the purchase of rare old books, must be connected with this area.

Mrs Huntingdon-Winstanley was watching him. 'Have you finished?' she asked.

'Not yet. I'd like permission to look over the entire apartment.'

'Why?'

'I like to be methodical.'

'Reasons for the method, Mr Samson. Give me reasons.'

Samson gave her a wearily reproachful look. 'You wouldn't expect a conjuror to tell you his secrets.'

'Ha! You're not a conjuror but we'll see how good you are at cards. See what sort of a card-sharp you make.'

She smiled displaying a gleaming row of false teeth in a sort of sideways sneer which reminded him of a shark.

'I'd like permission to look over your apartment,' he repeated.

'And you shall have it, but first you must pay a price and the price is a game of knockout whist.' Her smile seemed fixed and Samson, now close to the table, and caught in a sort of fascinated repulsion by the grimace, noticed a faint blue line on the margin between gum and teeth. Aware of his attention she snapped her mouth shut, only to open it a moment later to say, 'Come on, be a sport. Just one little game and then you can explore to your heart's content, although for the life of me I don't know what good it will do you, or me for that matter.' She rapped the table-top. 'Sit down.'

Samson thought of Georgia waiting outside. By the time

they returned to the office she might have found that working for a private investigator was less than glamorous.

'Do you know the rules?' asked Mrs Huntingdon-Winstanley, and without waiting for a reply went on, 'After cutting for deal we start with seven cards each. The dealer cuts the rest of the pack for trumps. It's the only time trumps are cut for. On following rounds the winner of the last round deals, turns up his or her last card and it is that suit which is trumps. Do you follow?'

'I've played the game before,' said Samson, settling himself on a small hard seat. 'We called it cut-throat whist when I was in the Navy.'

'You were in the Navy? My uncle was an admiral. Vice-admiral, actually. Admiral Henry Jameson. Uncle on my mother's side. Did you know him?'

'No.'

'You were lower deck, I imagine?'

'Yes.'

'Ah, well . . . Let's cut for deal. Aces high.'

With slightly trembling hand she cut the deck of cards. She had the eight of spades. Samson cut the six of diamonds.

'My deal,' she said. 'Now I'll cut for trumps.' She cut again and held up the queen of hearts. 'Hearts are trumps. Would you care to shuffle?'

Samson took the pack, gave a brief shuffle and handed the cards to the woman who was his client and opponent. She dealt seven cards to each. He picked up his hand. He had only two small hearts, and the only court card was the jack of diamonds. This suited him. So much the better if he was knocked out in the first round; he could continue with the work in hand.

He led the jack. She put down a ten. He took the trick and it was the only trick he took in that hand.

'Just six cards this time,' she said, 'and I turn up my last card and that is trumps. Such an unfair game I always

110

think. That's why I like it. I like unfair advantages in my favour and hate it when they're against me.'

While she was dealing six cards each Samson said, 'When your husband visits France, and comes back with books he's bought, he usually brings something for you. So you told me.'

'That's right. He does.'

'What sort of gifts does he bring?'

She bridled slightly. 'That's a very personal question.'

'No offence intended.'

'I'm sure it's not . . . Hearts are trumps again.'

Samson held a very good hand. Perhaps he could win outright and finish the charade. He led the ace of hearts and drew her only trump. He took every trick until the sixth and last when she placed the seven of clubs on his six.

'Aren't you going to tell me what sort of presents your husband brings back from abroad?' he asked.

'Why not. He brings me feminine things. They wouldn't be of any use to someone like you, Mr Samson. Beauty aids, scents. Incidentally, do you say "scents" or "perfumes"?'

'Perfumes,' replied Samson.

She shook her head disapprovingly. 'I expected as much. Perfume is a word shop-girls and the lower classes use. Or they did in my day. . . . You won that round. It's your deal.'

As he dealt five cards each Samson said, 'I was interested to hear you liked a vegetarian diet and prepared your own meals. What do you eat?'

He turned up the last card. The ace of spades.

'That's at least one trick to you,' she said. 'What do I eat? I start with muesli and bran for roughage.' She looked directly at him. 'I don't know why I should tell you this, but I quite like you.' The suggestion of a simper crossed her painted face, and she lowered her voice to a whisper. 'It's very intimate, but I find it difficult to do, well, you know what.'

'Constipation?'

She shuddered. 'Dreadful word. But yes. And I have plenty of what the common man would call "rabbit food". For protein I have wholemeal bread, fresh fish and, my favourite, lentil soup. I make it myself.' Her mouth began to water. 'Lentils, split peas, pearl barley, carrots, tomato pureé, marrow fat peas, yellow peas, a whole onion, garlic, bay leaves, chicken stock and a touch of fresh herbs. I grow the herbs in window-boxes.'

'Sounds good,' said Samson, and he meant it. He then played his ace of trumps on her lead of a small club. 'Where do you get your fish?' he asked.

'I don't *get* it. It is *delivered* by a fishmonger. I like smoked fish, particularly smoked trout. Smoked trout with a slice of wholemeal bread spread with unsalted butter. Delicious!'

She was salivating freely. Samson found it revolting and concentrated on his hand of cards. 'How many meals a day?' he asked.

'One main meal. Plenty of fruit juice. Vitamin C is most important although the quacks will tell you that you excrete any surplus. I don't believe them. I abide by vitamin C.'

As the hand closed with Mrs Huntingdon-Winstanley taking three tricks to Samson's two he asked, 'Do you take a lot of vitamins?'

'Certainly. I have any number. And I take Seatone. That's for my arthritis. An extract from a special sort of seaweed, as perhaps you know.'

She dealt four cards each and turned up her last card. The two of spades.

'Spades are trumps,' she announced.

Samson looked at his hand. He had two high spades, but he didn't win outright. He took three tricks to her one.

'You deal,' she said.

He shuffled the cards. 'What puzzles me,' he said, 'is

112

how someone seems to know all about my movements. Have you any ideas about that?'

'I don't trust that new girl.'

'Your maid?'

'Yes, her of the dreadful spectacles. I've seen her rolling her eyes at Simon. Much good it will do her.'

Samson turned up the last of his three cards. 'Clubs,' he said. It suddenly occurred to him that if he won outright she might demand another game to even the score. But he took the first and last trick in spite of trying to lose all three. The next round was down to two cards each.

'Why don't you trust your maid?' he asked.

'She slinks about so quietly. And it's not just that.' She studied the two cards in her hand. 'But I don't want to discuss it at the moment. I must concentrate. Which one of these shall I lead? . . . Let's try you with this.'

She placed the jack of spades on the table.

Samson laid down the three of spades.

'Ha!' she exclaimed. 'So I made a trick. The last is yours. I don't have a trump.'

She took the deck of cards and shuffled. 'This time it's one each but we have to cut for who deals. The dealer will automatically get a trump which gives a tremendous advantage.' She put the deck down on the table. 'Would you care to cut?'

Samson's hand dipped and he produced the ten of hearts.

'That's going to be hard to beat,' she said. Her card was the four of hearts. 'Your deal,' she said in an aggrieved tone. 'Now you're almost bound to win.'

Samson took the cards and began a quick shuffle. It wasn't difficult with practice and dexterity, to bring a couple of desired cards to the top of the pack, and in his youth he had learned a few tricks with cards.

The shuffle completed he gave Mrs Huntingdon-Winstanley her card and then put his own, face up, on the table. It was the eight of diamonds.

'The chances of beating that are too long,' said Mrs Huntingdon-Winstanley despondently as she flipped over her card. It was the nine of diamonds. 'I've won,' she exclaimed with childish delight. 'Didn't I tell you nine was my lucky number!'

'Well, they do say diamonds are a girl's best friend.'

'Oh, Mr Samson,' she crooned, 'I'm hardly a girl.'

He stood up. 'I'll have a look around, if I may.'

'Don't you want your revenge? Another game?'

He wagged an admonitory finger at her. 'Just one game. You said that was the price I had to pay.'

A petulent look crossed her face. 'Oh, all right then. Where do you want to start?'

Samson unstrapped his bag. 'I'll start in here.'

'What's that?' she asked as he produced an unfamiliar piece of equipment.

'I use it for sweeping.'

'Sweeping? You can't mean vacuuming?'

Samson was already moving around the room. 'This detects any hidden electronic device.'

'What they call a bug?'

'Exactly.'

'What makes you think there might be one in here?'

'I'm simply checking that there isn't,' he said, moving slowly around.

She watched as he completed a circuit of the room.

After putting the scanner back in his bag he took out a screwdriver and crossed the room to where a telephone stood on a Sheraton side table. With a few deft movements he dismantled the instrument sufficiently for his purpose.

'It's clean,' he remarked.

'I'm glad to hear of it. I assume you are eliminating possibilities of my conversations being overheard or recorded.'

'That's correct.' He returned to the table in the centre of the room. 'And now I'd like— ' He broke off. Mrs

Huntingdon-Winstanley was clasping her forehead with one hand and her head was nodding. 'Are you feeling unwell?' he asked.

'No. I'm all right. The excitement of the game is catching up with me.' Without removing the hand from her forehead she said, 'What do you want to do now?'

'I'd like to look round the rest of your apartment.'

'To see if there are any bugs?'

'Yes.'

She made to rise from her chair but slumped back again. 'I ought to come with you,' she said, 'but I don't really feel up to it at the moment.'

'Do you mind if I go on my own?'

She took the hand from her forehead and made a swatting motion. 'You do what you want. I trust you not to appropriate the family silver.'

Samson picked up his bag. 'I shan't be long,' he said.

Glad to be able to roam freely, he moved from room to room. As in most two-floor apartments the sleeping quarters were above the living quarters. Samson went upstairs.

The maid's room was small and furnished barely. Framed photographs lined the top of a chest of drawers and Samson noticed a small bottle containing sleeping pills on a bedside table. After slipping on light surgical gloves he had a cursory look through a small wardrobe and then moved next door to a bathroom.

The bedroom on the other side of the bathroom was locked. Not only was a key needed to open the door but it was also necessary to operate a four-digit security lock. Not having time to break the code Samson moved on.

The next bedroom was large and had an *en suite* bathroom. This was obviously where Mrs Huntingdon-Winstanley slept. The room contained a profusion of pink frills and flounces and was the acme of sugared femininity. He went to a kidney-shaped dressing table which was

115

covered by a variety of make-up aids. He tried the top drawers. These were locked. Mrs Huntingdon-Winstanley had evidently taken certain precautions before his arrival. Perhaps she had guessed he might want to snoop around.

He looked at jars of different shapes and sizes. Something about them wasn't quite right and it was a few moments before he realised what made them unusual. Apart from a jar labelled 'Collagen Cream' all the others, also containing creams, were unmarked by a house name, trade name or logo, and there was no indication of the nature of the jar's contents. Presumably Mrs Huntingdon-Winstanley could tell which cream was useful for what purpose by the shape of the jar.

He examined some cases of lipstick. Here again, except for one case marked 'Charles of the Ritz' there was no indication of their provenance. Samson tried to remember what Shandy's lipstick case looked like; he felt sure it had some distinguishing markings on it.

At one end of the dressing table was a small flat square box which had a glittering light metallic top. The letters YSL were embossed on the black and red background. Even though his knowledge of cosmetics was limited Samson knew the initials must stand for Yves Saint-Laurent, the one time protégé of Christian Dior.

Still wearing surgical gloves he pressed one side of the box and a palette slid out. It was like a miniature paint-box and contained various colouring agents which Samson assumed were for enhancing the beauty of eyes, lips and cheeks. There was also a small brush, presumably for the application of some of the contents of the box all of which were in pristine condition. A note at the top of the palette read: 'A little souvenir from France for your dressing table, with my love, Simon.' Had the little souvenir, Samson wondered, been too precious to spoil by use?

He replaced the box carefully and looked through the remaining items of make-up on the dressing table. There were powder puffs, mascaras, eye make-up remover, bottles of Arpège, Blue Grass and 4711 ('perfume' or 'scent'? Samson wondered) and rouge, and all were marked with trade names. So why were the lipsticks and creams mostly unmarked? He slipped a jar of cream and a lipstick case into his bag. He hoped Mrs Huntingdon-Winstanley wouldn't notice that among so many beauty aids only two were missing. Less valuable than the family silver, he thought.

Next he examined a telephone by the bed. It was bug free.

A built-in wardrobe with three sliding glass doors lined one wall. Samson slid back each door in turn. There were rows of dresses and four fur coats. A row of shoes, mostly flat-heeled, lined the floor of the wardrobe.

From the bedroom he went to the *en suite* bathroom which was decorated in coral pink and dove grey. He noted tins of talcum powder on a shelf all bearing some mark of their origin. There was also a plastic bottle containing a pink fluid and marked 'Sainsbury's moisturising foam bath'. A slight smile lightened Samson's features as he reflected that Sainsbury's chain of supermarkets was some way down-market from Charles of the Ritz and Yves Saint-Laurent. But Mrs Huntingdon-Winstanley's tastes were unpredictable. He would never have dreamed that a woman whose sitting room was filled with valuable antique furniture and staid portraits in oils would have a bedroom of stunning tastelessness, and he wouldn't have guessed either that someone who appeared cultured should be addicted to romantic novels.

A large mirror-fronted cabinet hung on the far wall above a bidet. Samson opened it. On the top shelf were two bottles of proprietary medicines which were popular cough mixtures, a packet of indigestion tablets, bottles of calamine lotion and witch hazel, a packet of aspirins, a bottle of eye lotion for soothing tired or sore eyes, a well-known laxative and an elegantly shaped pink glass jar. Attached to the lid of the jar was a thin reed-like stalk. Samson unscrewed the lid and saw the jar contained a greyish powder. He sniffed. It was odourless. After taking an envelope from his bag he tipped out a small quantity of powder. He sealed the envelope and put it away. He then took out a camera and photographed the contents of the cabinet.

Next he looked at the second shelf which housed powder for cleaning artificial teeth, an aerosol of dry shampoo for wig cleaning, a safety razor with a long, carved bone handle, a shaving brush marked 'Taylor of Bond Street' and a white plastic jar similarly marked but with the additional words 'Herbal Aromatics – Shave Cream'. Samson unscrewed the lid and smelled the cream which bore the unmistakable odour of almonds. He screwed back the lid and replaced the jar in the cabinet. It was evident that Mrs Huntingdon–Winstanley preferred old-fashioned methods of depilation.

The only other item in the cabinet was a rubber syringe with a ball in the centre and a soft rubber nozzle which Samson recognised as an instrument for purgative enemas.

He closed the cabinet door.

Only a bin in a corner of the bathroom remained to be examined. He lifted the lid and found the bin empty.

Picking up his bag he returned to the landing. There was one more door and it had a security lock with a four-digit coding device near the handle. Presumably the two locked rooms belonged to Simon Winstanley and Robert Mansour and were out of bounds to everyone.

Having inspected the top floor Samson went down to the lower level. He entered a dining room which looked as though it was never used and contained a Hepplewhite sideboard with wing-cupboards and a Chippendale mahogany table. Silver candlesticks gleamed and an epergne was filled with fresh fruit but the effect of genteel and gracious living was offset by the presence of a modern hostess trolley.

Next Samson went to the adjoining kitchen. It was modern and spotlessly clean. He opened the door of a refrigerator which contained most of the usual foodstuffs including a number of cartons of yoghurt. Cupboards, when opened, revealed that many varieties of health food were available including herbal teas, and in one section of the kitchen a row of jars contained different mineral and vitamin supplements.

A utility room and a small lavatory were on conventional lines.

He went back to the sitting room and rejoined Mrs Huntingdon-Winstanley.

'Well,' she asked, 'are you any the wiser?'

'Are you feeling better?' he replied.

'Much better, thank you.'

'I'm not wiser,' he said, 'but I'm more curious.'

Her blue eyes sparkled. 'Do tell me. There are no cats around here to be killed by curiosity.'

'Two of the upstairs rooms have security locks. Why is that?'

'I told you they sometimes behave like a couple of boys. So childish really. Who cares what they keep in their rooms? I don't.'

Samson raised his eyebrows slightly like some pachyderm coming out of slumber. 'Surely the rooms aren't locked all the time?'

'I haven't any idea about Robert's. He is expected to look after his own quarters except for changing linen and personal laundry. As for Simon, I'm seldom around when his room is attended to each day. But the rooms are kept locked while they are abroad.'

'Why is that?'

'I admit it does seem a bit strange. I do hope Simon

isn't mixed up in anything like' – she hesitated – 'drugs.'

She gave an enquiringly guileful look and Samson wondered whether she had invented a morsel of information to hold his interest.

'Have you any reason to think that a drugs connection might be involved?' he asked.

'I have very sharp hearing. Excellent for one of my years. Not long ago, just as they were leaving to go somewhere I heard Simon ask Robert whether he had the coke. At least, that's what it sounded like. I know enough about this wicked world to guess that he wasn't referring to solid fuel or Coca-Cola.'

'You never mentioned this before.'

'It slipped my mind,' she said tetchily.

'Previously you told me you were worried your husband might be involved in an illegal activity because he'd met a criminal in or near Hyde Park. Now you mention drugs. Are there any other illegal activities you can think of?'

She gave an angry glare and sat up absolutely straight in a posture of regal disapproval. 'Really, Mr Samson! I much object to being cross-examined!'

'This isn't a cross-examination,' Samson began patiently but he never finished the sentence. Mrs Huntingdon-Winstanley had crumpled and seemed to be in the grip of convulsions. Her arms and shoulders jerked in violent involuntary contractions.

Once before, when dealing with a divorce case, Samson had a client who suffered an epileptic fit in his office. He and Shandy had laid the man on the floor and Shandy had loosened his tie and collar. Samson, whose medical knowledge was limited, decided to copy the treatment.

He lifted the unconscious Mrs Huntingdon-Winstanley bodily from her chair, an effort needing considerable strength, and deposited her on her back on a clear part of the carpet. He then loosened a belt round her waist and straightened her wig. He was about to dash to the telephone to make an emergency call for an ambulance when the convulsions stopped and she opened her eyes. From her prone position she looked up at him and screamed. It wasn't the reaction he had expected. He went down on one knee beside her. 'No need for that. Please!' It flashed through his mind that if she became hysterical the treatment was a sharp slap in the face. 'Please!' he begged.

She stopped screaming and her hands went down to the part of her dress which covered her thighs. She fumbled at the material, pulling it down.

'You've interfered with me!'

'I have not interfered with you, madam!'

Her arthritic fingers played with the loosened belt.

'Why is this undone?'

'You were unconscious. You had some sort of fit. I was trying to give first aid.'

'Fit? Nonsense. I don't have fits.'

Samson stood up. 'I'm going to ring for medical help.'

'You'll do nothing of the sort. I won't have a doctor here.' She half sat up and with one hand felt for her wig. Reassured that it was in place and hadn't slipped she said, 'Help me to my feet and stop behaving like a panicky man.'

As gently as he could Samson hoisted her up and led her to her chair by the table.

'Now then,' she said. 'What were we talking about?' Before he could reply she went on, 'I remember. It was some sort of cross-examination.'

'Not a cross-examination, but I have to ask questions.'

'Oh, all right,' she said petulantly. 'Go on. Ask away.'

'Apart from a chance remark you overheard, have you any other reason to think drugs might be involved?'

She looked straight ahead. 'No, sir.'

'Apart from that, and the knowledge that your husband had one meeting with a member of the criminal fraternity, you have no cause to think he may be involved in an illegal activity?'

Continuing to look straight ahead and not at him she replied crisply, 'No, sir.'

'When you 'phoned me to say the birds had flown the nest did you have an idea where they might have gone?'

'No, sir,' she replied, holding herself rigidly erect.

'Presumably to France.'

'Presumably, sir,' she replied, still staring straight ahead and not moving a muscle.

Samson sighed. She was playing games again, pretending to be a witness under cross-examination by a bullying counsel.

'Mrs Huntingdon-Winstanley?'

'Sir?'

'Unless you stop playing childish games I shall withdraw from this case.'

She relaxed her posture and gave her slanting smile. 'Ha! It took you long enough to say that, didn't it?'

Samson picked up his bag.

'I've had enough of this charade,' he said, 'I'm going.'

Suddenly she attempted to become feminine and yielding. It was a grotesque exhibition. 'How I admire a man who is a real man,' she simpered, 'and speaks with authority. You may be of rather common stock, Mr Samson, but I'm beginning to admire you. Please, please don't go. You will be amply rewarded, I promise you.'

'Money has nothing— ' he began.

She interrupted with, 'We will not discuss money. I am prepared to pay whatever you ask and that's the end of the matter. Have you any other questions? I'm beginning to feel a little tired.' She passed her hand over her forehead. 'It must have been that little faint I had.'

'Do you know the combinations which open the doors of the two upstairs bedrooms?'

'No, of course I don't, and I don't wish to. What

makes you think I'd want to go into either bedroom!'
She shuddered. 'The very thought!'

'You don't know how long they'll be away?'

'No, Simon never tells me, but I'm a bit of a detective myself. I noticed they were travelling with light hand-baggage.'

'When your husband makes telephone calls does he usually make them from here or somewhere else in the house?'

'I can't really answer that. He makes some calls from downstairs but he must make a lot from his room. I wouldn't know. I see my own telephone bill before it goes to my accountant, but not his.'

'You have separate bills?'

'Of course we do. Most of the 'phones in the apartment are under my number but the 'phone in his room has a different number, ex-directory like mine. But I believe he also has a 'phone using my line.'

Samson assimilated the information. It was clear that while Winstanley could listen to all the calls she made, she couldn't listen to his calls if he used the line for which he paid the bills.

'Can you tell me your husband's private number?' he asked.

'I haven't the faintest idea what it is,' she replied loftily. 'Why, in heaven's name, should I wish to ring him up when I never leave the apartment? Really, Mr Samson, you do ask some absurd questions. It's all very tiring.'

'I'm sorry you're feeling tired but there is one more question I'd like to ask.'

'Go ahead, if you must.'

'You may sometimes have conversations with your husband.'

Samson waited for her comment.

'Is that a question? Of course we have conversations. And when he's in a good mood we have a game of spillikins.

123

Further, strange as it may seem, we both enjoy programmes on the television called *Coronation Street* and *EastEnders*. The characters are quite fascinating in a ghastly sort of way. Do people like that really exist, do you think?'

'I expect so, but I'm not an *aficionado* of either programme.'

'"I'm not an *aficionado* of either programme",' she mimicked in a gruff voice.

Samson ignored the mimicry. 'In conversations does your husband ever mention the Loire valley or towns on the Loire?'

She thought. 'Strange you should ask that. He's recently developed a taste for Balzac and says he visited some of the places where Balzac set his novels. They were in the Touraine region of the Loire.'

'One supplementary question.'

'Go ahead.'

'How long has your husband regularly been visiting France?'

'Oh, I don't know. Regularly, about two or three years. My memory isn't very good for recent events. Maybe four.'

'Thank you.' Samson began moving towards the door. 'I'll see myself out.'

'You'll leave the way you came?'

'Yes.'

She stood up. 'Wait for me. I want to watch. It's quite exciting. . . . You're sure you didn't touch me?'

'I touched you but I didn't molest you.'

'Ha! A nice distinction.' Gripping her stick she hobbled after him to the door.

Progress up the stairs to the landing and fire escape was slow.

'When they built this place they didn't take the lift shaft to the very top,' she complained. 'A stupid piece of planning. It means I have to climb stairs.'

Samson stood back to allow his client to go ahead.

124

When she reached the top of the stairs she paused. 'I tire so easily these days,' she said. 'And don't tell me it's my age.'

'Even a lower-deck man wouldn't be so discourteous.'

'Ha! So that got home, did it?' She began moving slowly forward and Samson noticed, as he had before, that her right foot seemed to droop. It looked as though at any moment she might trip up. He was watching the foot with some concern when she said, 'I do really quite like you, Mr Samson. It may surprise you, but I'm usually quite shy, even timid, with strangers, and yet I haven't felt like that with you. Strange, isn't it?'

Before he could think of a suitable reply she continued, 'That's one reason why I hate going out. And the thought of eating in public . . . Well, it's unthinkable.'

They reached the fire-escape door.

'Goodbye Mrs Huntingdon-Winstanley. I'll continue working on this matter but it's better that you contact me rather than that I get in touch with you. Give me a call when you're on your own and after your husband has returned.'

'Thank you.' She hesitated. 'I feel awful about not offering you a cup of tea or something but really, with Jennifer away, it's difficult for me to manage. Forgive my apparent lack of hospitality.'

'Think nothing of it,' Samson replied as he opened the door and let himself out.

125

Chapter 9

Georgia greeted him with, 'Am I glad to see you.'

'Problems?'

'Nothing I couldn't handle. Family of tourists in a Dormobile looking for the zoo, the police and two punters.'

'What did the police want?'

They were walking towards the main road where Samson hoped to hail a taxi.

'They were watching me. Didn't you notice the car parked at the top of the street?'

'You signalled that it was all clear.'

'They were watching me. They passed me twice and stared out and then they parked at the end of the street. I reckon they thought I was on the game and were waiting to pounce. I'd already had two men in cars ask if I was free for a bit of fun. I reckon one more and the cops would have moved in, and then where would you have been? Stranded at the top of a fire escape.'

'You did well.'

'How about you?' She looked up at him and quickened her pace to match his. 'Any joy?'

'Some. Tell you later.'

They reached the main road and within two minutes were taxi-borne to Samson's office.

It wasn't until late in the day, and the office closed, that he was able to discuss the case with Shandy. Seated in a new leather captain's-style swivel-chair in front of a new large leather-topped desk made of yew wood, Samson looked more like a successful businessman than he ever had at his former office. Instead of a row of antique clocks he now faced a magnolia-wash wall on which were two large oil paintings by marine artists of harbour scenes. A bookcase was half filled with new reference books and, inevitably, there was a cocktail cabinet for his liquid refreshment. Windows were double-glazed and had lined curtains which complemented the thick pile of a beige and brown carpet. Seats for clients were leather upholstered in the same shade of dark green as Samson's chair and desk top.

3handy took one of these chairs and sat beside Samson as he outlined details of the meeting with Mrs Huntingdon-Winstanley. He concluded, 'She seemed to think there might be a drugs connection, but I'm not sure she wasn't trying something on, a new game maybe. I don't sense the scene is a drugs one. But leave that aside, I'd like to pick your brains on cosmetics.'

'Pick away.'

'Is it usual for creams to be unlabelled like hers were, all except for one marked "Collagen Cream"?'

'No, it isn't. Collagen, incidentally, is supposed to replace ageing cells.'

'What might the others be used for?'

Shandy wrinkled her forehead. 'Difficult to say. Could be foundation cream, cleansing cream, protective cream, cream with vitamin E, cream with royal jelly, medicated cream or ointment – there are all sorts of creams.'

'What about lipsticks? Are they usually labelled?'

'They should carry a note of the colour.'

'I thought so.' Samson reached into his bag. 'What do you make of this?' he asked, handing her the envelope containing grey powder. 'It was in a pretty pink jar. The lid of the jar had a thin stalk with a fine brush-like tip.'

As he had done, Shandy sniffed the powder. 'It's a guess,' she said, 'but it might be some sort of eye-liner although it's an unusual colour. If I'm right, and it's something to do with eye make-up, the thin stalk would be an applicator.'

Samson placed a jar of cream and a lipstick on the side of the desk. 'I'd like you to get Jim Wilson to analyse these for me.'

She gave him a quick, searching look. 'Have you got any theories?'

'Yes, but don't ask me what they are. Theories without facts aren't much better than daydreams.'

Shandy changed the conversation. 'How did Georgia shape up today?'

'She was all right. Did her bit as look-out.'

'I rather missed going out with you,' said Shandy wistfully. 'I hope she isn't going to take all the jobs when you need someone.'

Samson reached out and patted her arm affectionately, but he said nothing.

Shandy picked up the jar of cream, the lipstick and the envelope containing grey powder. 'I'll get these to Jim but you may have to wait. I know he's hellishly busy.'

'Offer him anything he wants. The sky's the limit. This must have top priority.'

'Bribe him, you mean? Bribe him to let us jump the queue?'

'Exactly.'

'Okay. Is there anything else you want or can I go home?'

'You go. I'll lock up.'

She was almost at the door when he spoke her name. She turned. 'Yes?'

'No one replaces you,' he said. 'You're irreplaceable.'

She smiled. 'That's nice to hear even if it's not strictly true.'

The telephone was ringing when he entered his flat. A split second before he touched the handset he sensed the caller would be Mrs Huntingdon-Winstanley. He was right.

'Mr Samson, I'm so sorry I made a fuss today. I don't know what came over me. But you must admit it is very disconcerting for a lady of my age to find herself on her back on the floor with a large man looming over her.'

'I hope you're feeling better.'

'I'm quite well, thank you. When one gets older one's heart doesn't always pump enough blood to the brain, and the brain lacking oxygen causes one to faint.'

'I understand.'

'It's nothing to worry about. Perhaps the excitement of the knockout whist was too much for me.'

'Perhaps. Was there anything else you wanted to tell me?'

'No, I don't think so. I simply wanted to apologise and explain although I know some people hold that one should never do either. I think that's rather bad manners. What are your views?'

Samson didn't want an exchange of opinions on bad manners, but he felt sorry for Mrs Huntingdon-Winstanley. She was a lonely old woman seeking the solace of some sort of human contact. It was pathetic that she should be so limited in her circle of acquaintances that she was driven to call him.

'Are you still there, Mr Samson?'

'Yes.'

'Why don't you speak then? I asked you a question.'

'Mrs Huntingdon-Winstanley, I've had a busy day and I really must ask you to excuse me.'

He heard the sound of a 'phone being slammed down. She had rung off on him. If this wasn't an example of bad manners, he wondered, what was?

The abrupt end to an unwanted call didn't worry him but he was becoming concerned about the state of his client's health. He felt sure she was a sick woman but the nature of her sickness was beyond him, although he

129

had the uneasy suspicion that some of the symptoms she showed might indicate a life-threatening condition.

He went to a vestibule near the front door and took off his coat. After hanging it up he returned to the sitting room and poured a stiff whisky. It was almost time for a television newscast. He switched on the set and sat down.

It was while he was watching an item about a train crash in Brazil that he noticed an ornament was missing from the top of a small walnut cabinet. It was a blue goblet of Murano glass which Shandy had given him on her return from her honeymoon in Venice and, although he wouldn't have admitted it, was of great sentimental value.

Its absence was puzzling. He had that same morning before leaving for the office paused to look at it and he knew it must have been in place earlier in the day. Only two other people had keys to his flat; Shandy, and a trusted woman, Mrs Collas, who came twice a week for housekeeping duties. Today wasn't the day for her regular visit.

No longer interested in world news, he switched off the television and went across to the cabinet. It seemed impossible that the ornament could have fallen behind the cabinet but nevertheless he crouched down and peered behind it. There was nothing to be seen.

He went all round the flat, looking everywhere, and yet all the time knowing he couldn't possibly find the object of his search. It was a futile exercise, on a par with looking for land in mid-Atlantic, and yet he continued, against all reason, to look in every corner. To himself he explained the pointlessness of the search by the conjecture that in a moment of aberration he had moved the ornament and had totally forgotten doing so. But he knew he had done no such thing. Before leaving that morning he had paused to look at the object, remembered Shandy's happiness on return from the honeymoon, her swift kiss on the cheek when she gave him the present, and had gone straight to the vestibule, put on his coat, opened the front door, closed and locked it, then walked to the lift.

He returned to the sitting room, finished his whisky, and sat in an armchair deep in thought. During his search he had looked to see if anything else was missing or whether there was evidence of a break-in. He had drawn a blank on both possibilities.

And yet someone must have entered, taken the blue goblet, and left. Why? It had little intrinsic value. It wasn't some rare and coveted collectable.

The following morning before leaving for the office he cooked eggs and bacon. It was when he tipped up the lid of the waste-disposal bin that he saw fragments of blue glass lying on top of kitchen refuse.

He picked out the fragments and laid them on a table oblivious to the frying eggs and bacon.

His appetite for breakfast vanished when finally he looked at hard yellow yolks and shrivelled cinders of bacon.

Someone had entered his flat on the previous day, picked up and deliberately smashed an ornament and gone. This wasn't a case of a peculiar theft. It was intimidation. Was someone letting him know that the interior of his flat was easily accessible?

He dispensed with breakfast except for a cup of coffee. While he drank it he tried to fathom who might want to break the goblet.

Names from the past floated in and out of his mind; none seemed to fit the offence. But one name recurred. It was Simon Winstanley who had known of his mandate and tried to buy him off. And yet it seemed highly improbable that Winstanley, who was abroad, would hire someone to perpetrate an act of vandalism.

He decided to eliminate his housekeeper from the problem and put through a call.

'Did you come to the flat at any time yesterday, Mrs Collas?'

'As a matter of fact, I did, sir. I'd left something behind when I left the day before. A bit of shopping. I'd put it in the cupboard near the front door while I hoovered the carpet and forgot to take it with me.'

'You didn't by any chance, by accident, break the blue glass goblet which stood on top of the cabinet?'

'No, sir. But when I collected my shopping I noticed something shining on the floor of your sitting room. I went to see what it was, and it was glass, lying in pieces on the carpet. I got the dustpan and brush and swept it up and put the bits in the bin.'

'It was broken before you arrived?'

'Oh, yes, sir. I didn't do it.'

'I'm sure you didn't.'

Before leaving for the office Samson decided that a burglar alarm must be installed as soon as possible. He had been the classic example of the expert who, while safeguarding the welfare of others, had ignored his own welfare.

When, later that day, he told Shandy what had happened she said, 'So you think someone may be getting at you? It couldn't be Mrs H-W, could it?'

'It must have happened before I went to see her and before she hung up on me during the evening.'

'I didn't mean that she could have done it personally. Or that it had anything to do with the interview. But you told me she likes playing games. Maybe this is another of her games and she's hired someone like you, a p. i. or a security man, to do it.'

Samson considered the proposition. 'Very unlikely. What is interesting is that you, like me, feel there's a connection with that particular case. But then people in our line of business are always looking for connections, for links between apparently unrelated events. We sometimes overlook the simple in a search for the complex. It's conceivable that the goblet could have been shattered by some high-pitched sound from outside.'

Shandy gave a smile. 'Never mind,' she said, 'Paul and I are planning to visit Florence in June and to make a sentimental day trip to Venice. I'll try to get you another.'

'It won't be the same,' said Samson sadly.

Chapter 10

Jim Wilson was a highly skilled technician, one of a team working in a forensic science laboratory. Samson had first met him eight years previously when Wilson suspected his wife was having a love affair and wanted her followed. His suspicions had been justified. Under pretence of taking evening classes in Spanish she was visiting a single man who lived in rooms above a hall where the classes were held.

When Jim Wilson confronted her with the evidence Samson had obtained, instead of showing contrition she launched a counter-attack on him for having employed a private detective. 'If you thought I was being unfaithful,' she had begun a tirade, 'why didn't you have it out with me direct, instead of being so underhand, so devious, so treacherous, as to invite someone to pry into our private lives?' She had grabbed a few clothes, stuffed them into a suitcase, and stormed out of the house.

Samson had then been sent to find her. She had not, as expected, gone to her lover but to a boarding house on the east coast run by a friend. Samson had spoken to her, told her that her husband loved her dearly, and had asked her to return. After a tearful scene in which she spoke of having been torn between two lovers she agreed. Samson effected a reconciliation in his office, playing the part of marriage guidance counsellor. The rift had been healed and some months later a first child was born. Samson had been invited to the christening.

Over the years he had kept in touch with Jim Wilson who, when Samson needed services requiring forensic expertise, would undertake extra-mural work on his behalf using laboratory facilities. The arrangement was on a strictly business basis with Samson paying in cash.

Two days after his meeting with Mrs Huntingdon-Winstanley Shandy came into his room. 'This has just arrived by special messenger,' she said, handing over a sealed envelope. 'It's from Jim. I imagine it's the report you wanted.'

Samson ripped open the envelope and began reading.

Dear John,

As you wanted a report in a hurry I haven't made a detailed analysis. If you need this, please let me know. Treat what follows simply as preliminary findings.

The jar of cream. It was helpful to be told this was for cosmetic purposes. The cream contains the normal constituents for cosmetic emollients. When Shandy spoke to me she wondered if the cream might contain lanolin. Lanolin is used to moisturise and protect. The sample you have provided is basically normal cleansing cream made from synthetic oil and water but there has been an additive to the cream. It contains mercury which is a prohibited substance because of its toxicity.

The lipstick. Here again the constituents are basically what lipstick should contain, i.e. wax to provide slip and gloss and pigments for colour. But the sample you have provided also contains a high proportion of lead. I should point out that where concentrations of lead are high one should suspect what is known as 'cosmetic plumbism'.

The grey powder. This was difficult. It was helpful to know it was probably for cosmetic purposes, eye-liner perhaps. I found it to be composed largely of lead sulphide. In view of the toxicity of the cream and the

135

lipstick I went to our library and looked up references to papers and originals in the *British Medical Journal*. In the issue of 30 September 1978 I found a fascinating article headed 'Surma and lead poisoning' contributed by Aulfat R. Ali, Oliver R. C. Smales and Mohamed Aslam. Surma is a fine powder either black, white or grey – the grey powder contains the highest proportion of lead – which is applied to the conjunctival surfaces of the eyes rather than the outside of the eyelids. The word 'surma' is derived from an Urdu word meaning 'antimony' but because antimony sulphide is in short supply the manufacturers use lead sulphide. Surma is available in this country and commonly used by Asian families for cosmetic purposes and to relieve eyestrain. In Pakistan it is purchased from a 'hakim', or healer. According to the article the Government has issued health warnings but even if there is legislation prohibiting sale of surma, in the opinion of the authors people will still be able to obtain it from abroad from friends, relatives or the hakim.

I hope this sketchy information is of some use. One doesn't have to be a detective to realise that somebody is trying to poison somebody through the use of cosmetics. I imagine this would be a slow process with minerals slowly building up in the body but you would have to ask you local friendly doctor about this.

Jenny asks me to send kindest regards. Amanda is doing well at school. As for the honorarium, forget it this time. This one is on me. It was a fascinating job and I hope that one day you'll tell me what it was all about.

Yours ever,
JIM

Samson handed the letter to Shandy. 'Read that.'
When she gave him back the letter she said, 'Isn't it

typical? When we've got a client who's willing to pay the earth, Jim does it for free. . . . Do you want me to call her?'

Samson considered her question for some moments before answering. 'I think I ought to warn her,' he said, 'but I don't want to put a stop on the case. I want to get to the bottom of what's going on. There's more involved than the poisoning of an old lady. I'd like to know who is supplying the cosmetics. But I mustn't delay too long before putting her in the picture.'

'Difficult decision?'

'Yes. Leave me to think about it.'

'Right. By the way, Georgia asked me to remind you that Mrs Cumbermack is here.'

'Not her again. Not more messages from outer space that need deciphering.'

'Probably.'

Samson gave a theatrical sigh. 'Ask Georgia to bring her up. Mrs H-W will have to wait for her salvation.'

It was late in the afternoon before Samson was able to devote his attention to Mrs Huntingdon-Winstanley's plight. Before taking any direct action to prevent what appeared to be a case of slow poisoning he thought he should check on the facts of metallic poisoning. All his reference books on medical matters had been destroyed by fire except for an old edition of *Black's Medical Dictionary*, and although this book was of some help he decided to discuss the salient points of the case with a doctor whom he knew socially.

Ewart Humphries was a retired general practitioner who, when Samson first met him, had lived alone in a bunga-low in the green belt surrounding London. He had been a self-sufficient man embedded in a daily routine which, when the weather allowed, included at least an hour in his garden and nine holes of golf and, without exception for weather or anything else, regular twice-weekly evening visits to a pub in north London.

And then he fell in love with and married a woman much younger than himself who was intelligent enough to accept and respect the differences between them and didn't try to alter his habits. His life-style changed very little except that the bungalow was sold and he and his wife moved into a larger house in the same district.

Samson paid a visit to the pub patronised by Ewart Humphries. It was a place cluttered with brass and copper ornaments offset by a wealth of oak beams. Recesses were filled with artificial flowers and a large stuffed grizzly bear stood in one corner. Someone had pinned a rosette bearing the colours of Tottenham Hotspur Football Club on the bear's chest and, with its partly opened jaws and outstretched paw the stuffed animal might have been a cheering supporter of the club waiting for a friend to hand it a drink.

When Samson entered the pub he saw Ewart Humphries seated in his customary corner opposite the bear. He was a distinguished-looking man with a mass of grey hair above a face which might have been used as a model by Praxiteles. After mutual greetings Samson elbowed his way to a crowded bar and returned with two large whiskies.

'Good to see you again,' said Humphries, 'but I'm too old in the tooth to think this is an accidental encounter. Right?'

'Right.'

'You're involved in a case which has a medical dimension?'

'Right again.'

'Well, I still keep reasonably *au fait* with things. I sift through the *Lancet*, the BMJ, and some of the bumf drug companies send even though I should be off their mailing list by now. . . . So, what's the problem?'

'Metallic poisoning, I think.' Samson went on to outline

the facts as they affected Mrs Huntingdon-Winstanley's health and her use of cosmetics but omitting reference to other aspects of the case. When he had finished he gave Humphries the letter he'd received from Jim Wilson. After reading in silence Humphries handed back the letter. 'Cosmetic plumbism and toxicity generally is a bit outside my field,' he said, 'but oddly enough I came across an instance recently when reading a biography of the artist, Reynolds. One of Reynolds's models was a former apprentice milliner who became a celebrated society prostitute. Her name was Kitty Fisher. The poor girl didn't live long. She died at the age of twenty-six, "a victim of cosmetics" according to a contemporary record. . . . Let me think. Give me a moment. Must stir up the old grey matter.'

Samson watched the other customers who were mostly younger than himself and certainly noisier. The hubbub of their chatter was compounded by pop music from stereo speakers and when Humphries began speaking again Samson had to lean forward so as not to miss a word.

'Lead isn't absorbed through the skin,' Humphries began, 'in fact there is a *lotio plumbi* which is used to treat bruises. But it is easy to ingest if you eat something which has been contaminated by fumes or drink water from leaded pipes or lick your fingers when you've been touching something containing lead. Women often eat off their lipstick and your client could perhaps have ingested lead that way. As for the surma, your friend's letter is most helpful. I've never heard of the stuff. But as I've said, lead isn't absorbed through the skin. However, I notice from the letter that the surma is applied to the surface of the eye. The lead would then automatically be absorbed through the mucous membrane in the eye. It would contribute to lead poisoning. Lead is very slowly excreted and accumulates in the body tissues.' Humphries paused. 'Will that do?'

'It's fine. What are the symptoms?'

'Constipation is one. And there's neuropathy, or nerve damage, especially what is known as "dropped foot". The foot hangs down and the sufferer looks as though he's going to stumble at any moment. The sufferer will probably be anaemic. Would those symptoms apply to your client?'

Samson had a memory flash of Mrs Huntingdon-Winstanley walking up the stairs to the fire escape, and he remembered the laxative tablets in the bathroom cabinet and her admission that she suffered from constipation. 'The symptoms fit,' he said.

Humphries looked at Samson's empty glass. 'Have another?'

'Drinks are on me tonight,' Samson replied. 'It'll go down to expenses,' he added, observing that Humphries was about to protest, 'so let's not argue about it. And while I'm fighting for a place at the bar perhaps you'd like to give another stir to the grey matter and let me know about mercury.'

'I'm beginning to feel like a messenger,' said Humphries with a grin. 'Don't kill me if you don't like the message.'

'You're no messenger to the gods,' replied Samson, pleased with himself for having spotted the allusion to Mercury.

When he returned minutes later with two glasses of whisky he capped the allusion with, 'Who's Mercury now? Cup-bearer to the gods!'

'Neat,' said Humphries. 'Do you think Mercury's winged hat made him a mad hatter?'

'Mad hatter?'

'Ah, I've got you there. Mercury was a liquid used in felt-making at one time and, because most mercury compounds are absorbed through the skin, people working with felt, principally hat-makers, contracted mercury poisoning. Hence the expressions "Mad as a hatter" and "Hatter's shakes".'

140

'My client's hands were shaking some of the time,' said Samson recalling the games of spillikins.

'Other symptoms are fatigue, memory loss, difficulty in concentrating.'

'I wouldn't fault her concentration.'

'The only other thing I can remember, and I'm going back to student days to dredge it up, is that a sufferer from mercury poisoning is often uneasy in the presence of strangers and a peculiarity is that he or she doesn't like eating in public. . . . Oh, and one further fact. In Japan people die from eating fish poisoned with mercury. It's called minamata disease. And that, my dear John Samson, is your lot. The old grey matter has no more to give.'

'It's given enough,' said Samson raising his glass in acknowledgement. 'I'm very grateful.'

'So what will you do? Warn her? Notify the police?'

'I shall have to warn her but it isn't a CID case yet.'

'She should see her GP.'

'She doesn't have one,' said Samson. 'She's strongly opposed to orthodox medicine.'

'More and more people are. Alternative medicine has a real foothold.'

The conversation turned to other matters and by the time Samson left the pub he was well satisfied with the evening's gathering of intelligence.

On the following morning he told Shandy what Dr Humphries had said about lead and mercury poisoning.

'What are you going to do?' she asked.

'I shall have to tell her even if it puts a stop on the case.'

'And you don't want that?'

'I'm still convinced there's more to this than just poisoning an old lady.'

'Shall I put through a call to her?'

Samson thought. 'Winstanley and Mansour may have returned. It's difficult. I don't want to tell her on the

141

'phone. This is better done face to face.' After further thought he went on, 'You make a call. If Winstanley or anyone but her answers just ring off. If she answers, ask for Mr Winstanley. If she tells you to hold on while she gets him, ring off. But if she says he isn't at home, say who you are and put her through to me.'

'What if she asks, "Who wants to speak to him?"'

'Say, "I'm trying to find out if he's at home. This is Mr Samson's secretary speaking." She's sharp enough to get the message and say, "You've got a wrong number" or some other get-out.'

'Are you sure you want me to do this, and not Georgia?'

Samson screwed up his face. It was an odd expression and as if he'd unexpectedly swallowed a lemon pip. 'I want you to do it,' he said.

'Good.' She turned and walked out of the room, her buttocks swaying very slightly. She didn't see him shake his head, the head-shaking of a man who knew he would never fully understand the psychology of women which, whatever feminists might shrill to the contrary, was different from male psychology.

Two minutes later her voice came over the intercom. 'Mrs Huntingdon-Winstanley for you.'

'Mrs Huntingdon-Winstanley?'

'Speaking. Is that Mr Samson?'

'It is. Are you alone?'

'I am.'

'No chance of being overheard?'

'I'm still in bed. I haven't felt too well this morning.'

'I'm sorry to hear that. I wanted to come and see you.'

'When?'

'Whenever is convenient.'

'In about an hour's time?'

'That would be all right.'

'I'll be up. It'll be sheer laziness on my part if I'm not. Will you be coming up the same way?'

142

'It would be better. But is Jennifer there?'

'She is.'

'Can you get rid of her? Send her out for something which can only be obtained in some outlying part of town?'

A pause. 'I could do. But when I send her out for something I usually send her by taxi and it doesn't take very long. Wait a minute. I'll tell her I'm economising and she must travel by public transport. That'll delay her. Leave it to me, Mr Samson. I'll see you in an hour's time.'

Again he took Georgia to act as look-out and received a glance from Shandy which inexplicably made him feel slightly guilty. Why, he wondered, when Shandy had approved of having an extra member of staff, should she now be behaving as though she were jealous. It wasn't logical.

On his way to Mrs Huntingdon-Winstanley's apartment he asked Georgia, 'Do you think men are more logical than women?'

'I don't know about that,' she replied, 'but the bright ones are usually brighter. They suss out a situation quicker.'

Samson wisely decided not to pursue the point.

As before, he climbed the fire escape and found the door at the top had been left open.

Mrs Huntingdon-Winstanley was waiting for him in the sitting room. It might have been that knowing of her predicament he thought her face more garishly painted than ever, while from her bedizened features her eyes shone with a lustre that now seemed unnatural.

'Welcome, Mr Samson, do come and join me. I'm feeling better now and just in the right mood for a game of knockout whist. I'm afraid my wretched hands won't permit me to challenge you to spillikins.'

She gazed at him with a voracious intensity which

made him wish he was anywhere but in the stultifying atmosphere of an oppressively familiar room.

'Mind you don't trip over the footstool,' she said with a laugh. 'Do you remember the first time you called? I thought to myself What a clumsy man, but you're not clumsy at all.'

He took a seat at the table opposite her. She pushed the deck of cards towards him. 'You shuffle. Men shuffle cards so much better than women, don't you think?'

'I haven't come here to play cards.'

'You haven't? What a disappointment. You surely wouldn't disappoint me, would you?'

'I've come on a serious matter.'

'Oh, don't be boring. Anything can be serious if you make it so. Don't be serious. Enjoy life. My, you do look an old grouch this morning. What *is* the matter with you?'

'It isn't me, Mrs Hunting— '

'It isn't I,' she corrected sharply.

'Mrs Huntingdon-Winstanley, where do you get your cosmetics from?'

'What a question! What business is it of yours?'

She began to tremble and Samson realised that the meeting was going to be even more difficult than he had anticipated.

'I think it is my business,' he said.

'And I think you are being arrogantly presumptive.'

'It concerns what you are employing me to do.'

'Ha! I'm employing you to find out what my husband gets up to, not to delve into the secrets of a lady's boudoir. I knew it was a mistake to let you wander loose around the place.'

Samson's heavy head was so sunken into his broad shoulders that it looked as though it might disappear altogether.

'I must ask again. Where do you get— '

'Very well,' she interrupted, 'be tedious if you must. Let's get it over and then we'll have a game. You want to know where my little beauty aids come from? I'll tell you. I obtain them from Harrods.'

'All of them?'

'What do you mean?'

'I have reason to believe the jars of creams on your dressing table don't come from Harrods or any other store.'

'Reason to believe! You sound like a stage policeman from some unspeakably boring farce,' she said scornfully.

'That may be,' he replied doggedly, 'but I need to know. Where do you get your face creams from?'

She sat very erect in her chair and glowered at him. 'If it's any business of yours, which I greatly doubt, I obtain them from a source in France.'

'I thought that might be so. Which source?'

He lifted his head and returned her stare. It was an eyeball to eyeball confrontation. Neither spoke, neither wavered from a fixed gaze. It was an unflinching battle of wills. Mrs Huntingdon-Winstanley's eyes began to water but she continued to look unblinkingly at him.

After a silence which seemed interminable she spoke.

'We used to play this game at school. It's quite good fun. Staring contests, we called them. I always won. I could outstare the other girls. The trick is to stare at a point between the other person's eyes, not directly at the eyes.'

'I know.'

He was beginning to despair that the confrontation which had become a ridiculous childish contest would ever end, but suddenly she lowered her eyes. 'All right, I throw in the towel. It's no disgrace to be beaten by a strong man, and you are a strong man, Mr Samson.' She gave her peculiar shark-like smile. 'Not good-looking, but strong.'

'Where do the jars of cream come from?'

'If you must know, my dearly beloved husband, my naughty goat, brings them back from France.'

'And the lipsticks?'

'You *are* being tedious,' she burst out and she beat the table-top with clenched fists like a small, spoiled child in a tantrum.

'He brings them from France too?'

'Yes, yes, yes, yes, yes, yes, yes, yes, yes, yes, yes, yes— '

His voice overrode the last three yeses. 'And the eye-applicator in a pink glass jar? That comes from France too?'

The yeses faded to a whisper. He knew he had gained ascendancy and, pressing home his advantage, he said, 'We'll come to the eye-applicator later. First, where does your husband get the stuff from?'

She wilted in her chair like some weird plant which has been seared by lightning.

'I've been a teeny bit untruthful,' she said in a faint voice. 'I've been a naughty girl. I pretended I didn't know why Simon should be calling on Dr Maurice. That was what the EastEnders would call a porky-pie. A lie. The truth is that the good doctor has sovereign remedies for those of us who are not so young as we were. He takes the essence of certain herbs – the formula is his secret – and mixes this with an emulsion of oil and water.' She met his eyes once more. 'I'm sorry, but it was a harmless deception. Don't be cross with me.'

'I'm not cross,' he replied gently, 'but I have to disillusion you. I've had one of the creams analysed.'

Her mouth sagged open. 'Analysed . . . I don't understand.'

'It's bad news, I'm afraid.'

Her jaw muscles tightened. She looked as if she was gearing herself up for battle once more. 'Bad news? Out with it, man. Don't shilly-shally.'

'The cream contains mercury.'

'Mercury isn't a herb.'

'That's my point.'

A trembling hand went to her throat. 'My God! Mercury can be absorbed through the skin.'

'Yes.'

Her hand dropped lifelessly and she swayed in her chair. 'In my handbag,' she whispered. 'Smelling salts.'

Samson leapt to his feet, hurried round the table, rummaged through a voluminous handbag and found a small phial. He unscrewed the cap and sniffed. A strong ammoniac smell assailed his nostrils. He handed the phial to her. 'Here,' he said pressing the phial into her hand.

For two or three minutes she seemed to hover in a semi-conscious state and then, to his immense relief, she put down the phial and said, 'That's better. Thank you.'

He resumed his seat. 'I realise it must be a terrible shock.'

'It is a shock. What can Dr Maurice hope to gain?'

'Dr Maurice might not gain.'

'What?'

'It might not be Dr Maurice who gains.'

'Mr Samson, I hope you don't think – you aren't implying – that Simon would be party to such a dreadful thing. I know Simon. He wouldn't hurt a fly. His trouble is that he's easily led, and can be led by the wrong sort of person. But he wouldn't hurt me. Not me, of all people. You haven't any proof that he knows what's in the cream, have you?'

'No proof that he knows, but— '

'But me no buts,' she interrupted. 'Of course he doesn't know. He's probably been duped into paying a lot of money although . . . I can't think . . . What has Dr Maurice to gain by poisoning me?'

'The lipstick was tainted too,' said Samson, 'and the eye application. That is something called surma and contains a high concentration of lead. It enters the system through the mucous membranes in the eyes.'

147

'Lead as well as mercury,' she exclaimed. And then, more reflectively, 'Lead as well as mercury. That could explain why I've been under the weather these last few months. But why, why, why?'

'That's what I want to find out.'

'Oh, Mr Samson, I'm so glad I met you.' She held out her hand across the table.

He hesitated momentarily before reaching out to grasp the offered hand.

'You are a good man,' she went on. 'I knew I could trust you. I took to you right from the start. It's not everyone I invite to play Spillikins, you know.'

Samson released his grip. 'Then it was a compliment.'

'It was indeed. And now you must continue to be my guardian angel and help me to my room. I must remove all that horrible stuff from my face.'

Chapter 11

She sat down in front of the dressing table. Samson stood behind her. Each looked at the other in the mirror.

'I never thought I'd allow a man, a man not my husband, into my bedroom,' she said. 'But needs must when the devil drives.'

It had been a difficult haul up the stairs and Samson had needed all his strength to support her tottering figure.

'When will the maid be back?' he asked.

'I sent her to Richmond to obtain a special sort of herbal tea. She won't be back for ages.'

'Will you be all right on your own?'

She turned to look up at him. 'Please don't leave me. Not just yet. Wait until I've got rid of this dreadful stuff. You can help.' She reached out for a bowl of cotton wool and then, taking a bottle of make-up remover, began the process of stripping the thick coating from her face.

Samson watched in fascination as cracks in withered skin slowly appeared. A woman already old was ageing before his eyes; only her eyes retained their brightness.

As she dabbed with balls of cotton wool she said, 'I know of only one instance of metallic poisoning. It happened years ago when I was a nurse in the NHS. A thermometer broke in a patient's mouth and he swallowed the mercury. I got the houseman at once. I seem to remember that he ordered that the stomach should be washed out with sodium bicarbonate.'

'You must have medical attention, Mrs Huntingdon-Winstanley.'

'I must not. Don't presume to tell me what I must or must not do. No doctors. I'll get well under my own steam.' She paused. 'I may call in a homeopathic practitioner I know. I'll think about it. Yes, I might try homeopathy. After all, what is good enough for our dear Queen should be good enough for me.'

More cracks and fissures appeared and the skin surface became blanched in patches. Stained balls of cotton wool were dropped into a small bin.

'You are a detective, Mr Samson. Why should this surgeon whom I have never met try to poison me?'

'He provided the cosmetics, probably under instructions.'

'Who would order such a thing? Not Simon. I wonder . . . Yes, I wonder. I know Robert hates me. He's been trying to steal Simon from me. He'd like me out of the way. I wouldn't put it past him to substitute poisoned goods for the genuine goods while Simon wasn't looking, substitute the impure for the pure. What do you think of that, eh?'

Samson thought it an unlikely hypothesis but didn't say so. Instead he said, 'I shall make it my business to find out who is guilty and why.'

Mrs Huntingdon-Winstanley paused from dabbing her face. 'You are a jewel,' she said.

Samson wasn't easily embarrassed but he felt embarrassed as he caught her gazing at his reflection in the mirror. Her scarlet lips were parted in a leer which split her blotched face like a bloody gash. He looked away.

'In a minute,' she said, 'I'll have to ask you to help me to the bathroom. I shall wash out my eyes.' She paused from dabbing her face and unexpectedly said, 'Can you name the seven deadly sins?'

Samson had, many years before, seen a French movie about the seven deadly sins. He could only remember the episode which dealt with gluttony. A tired wayfarer had turned up at a run-down isolated farm seeking shelter. The farmer, a dull uncouth fellow, and his wife, a very attractive young woman, had taken pity on the wayfarer and invited him into their house. But the only food available was a huge cheese. The wayfarer had a slice, pronounced it good, and had another. He was offered a bed for the night which, because it was the only bed in the house, happened to be the matrimonial bed. On retiring the husband took one side, the wife took the central position, and the wayfarer took the other side. The husband was soon soundly asleep. Turning seductively to the wayfarer the wife asked if there was anything he would like to have and she moved her body suggestively. 'There is something I would like' said the wayfarer, 'I'd like another slice of that delicious cheese.'

This episode had greatly appealed to Samson who wasn't free from the deadly sin of gluttony. It was, in fact, the only episode in the movie which he remembered. In reply to Mrs Huntingdon-Winstanley's question he said, 'Gluttony.'

'That's one. Name the other six.'

'Sloth.' This was another sin with which he was familiar.

'That's two. Five to go.'

'Lust.' He had lusted, but not often, and certainly not for the woman whose face seemed to be slowly peeling like the decaying façade of an old, neglected house.

'Go on,' she said. 'You've named three.'

Was this another game? he wondered.

'Pride.' He took pride in his work but had never been guilty of the pride which is an excessive conceit.

'Four.'

'And there's anger,' he said naming a deadly sin of which he wasn't completely guiltless.

'Five.'

'Avarice.' Samson's acquaintance with poverty as a child had made him determined never to be poor as an adult, but he wasn't greedy for riches. 'And envy,' he concluded, naming the deadly sin which at some time and place must have touched every human being.

'Very good. Now I'm going to add an eighth. It's been my downfall. Do you know what it is?'

'I've no idea.'

'Vanity,' she said. 'That's the eighth deadly sin. It's the sin of narcissism.'

Her face was now almost clear of the carapace of cosmetics and every crease and wrinkle cruelly exposed in criss-crossing lines which covered nearly every inch of a sallow skin.

'Vanity of vanities,' she sighed. 'Our passions sometimes leave us at rest but vanity agitates us constantly, as some philosopher once said. Was it La Rochefoucauld? I don't know. My memory's going.' She staggered to her feet. 'Now help me to the bathroom, will you?'

Samson held her arm as she teetered, one foot dropped, clasping her stick like a talisman, into the bathroom. With an eye-bath she washed out both eyes.

'What a terrible thing to do,' she said, 'to poison someone through their eyes. Get that bottle of what's-its-name, Mr Samson, and throw it away.'

'The surma might be needed as evidence. It must be left. You didn't know the properties of surma?'

'I did not. Simon told me that Dr Maurice had recommended the stuff as an aid to making one's eyes lustrous.' She put down the eye-bath. 'On no account must you inform the police of this. I couldn't bear the scandal.'

'The police will have to be notified eventually. A crime has been committed.'

'By Robert, yes. I want you to find proof that Robert has tried to kill me, and without Simon's knowledge.' She began to tremble. 'No,' she breathed. 'No, I won't!' The trembling passed. 'Will power,' she said. 'Mind over matter.' She got to her feet and began to stagger back towards the bedroom. Samson held her free arm. 'No

152

doctors and no police,' she said. 'Is that understood?'

'I hear you.'

'I shall stay in my room until Jennifer gets back. You'll have to see yourself out.'

Samson assisted her to the bed with its valanced pink silk bedspread. She slumped heavily on its side and, waving her stick dismissively, said, 'You can go now. I'll let you know when there's something to report. Thank you for your help today. You won't go unrewarded. Now leave.'

Samson felt a surge of the deadly sin of pride. His pride resented patronage. 'Good day, Mrs Huntingdon-Winstanley,' he said and he walked swiftly from the room.

When he rejoined Georgia she said, 'Don't look now but we're being watched.'

'By whom?' he asked as they walked down the road.

'I think it's the police. The car is unmarked but the men inside look like cops. It's a re-run of what happened before. They went past, came back, and now they're parked at the end of the street.'

'Strange.'

'I'd say it was spooky.'

Samson glanced sideways at the pert figure beside him dressed in a light green velour leisure suit. 'Do you mind?' he asked.

'Mind? I love it. It beats the dole.'

As they reached the end of the road Samson looked round. A car was moving slowly forward. 'Wait here,' he said. Then, moving quickly he advanced towards the car. As he approached, it accelerated and drove past him. The men inside were looking straight ahead.

Samson knew he was taking a chance in changing the venue of his office. In south London he had built up a profitable business and was concerned lest the move might result in a falling off of custom. It was gratifying to find that

153

business opportunities were increasing. West End lawyers were seeking his services and since his name-plate had appeared there had been callers from clubland. His latest caller was a top civil servant who was being blackmailed by a prostitute's pimp. The civil servant refused to go to the police and wanted Samson to act as intermediary. After the interview was finished he sent for Shandy who was now in sole charge of minor cases. It had always been his habit to discuss the difficult cases with her and he saw no reason to change.

After relating the morning's events he said, 'I'm not convinced that the only motive for poisoning her cosmetics is so that Winstanley can get his hands on an inheritance. From what she said at our first meeting he's building up an income from his own efforts, whatever those may be.'

'Do you think it's Robert's doing? That he's switching creams and lipsticks?'

'I'd like to know a lot more about Dr Maurice.'

'I have checked the Medical Directory. His name doesn't appear.'

'I've been thinking about that,' said Samson. 'It could be that the garage mechanic in Nonancourt who said he was a foreigner who'd arrived only a few years ago was speaking in a parochial sense. Maurice might, for example, be a native of Alsace-Lorraine. . . . I'll try Anton. See whether he can come up with anything.'

Anton was an old friend of Samson's and in the same line of business. He had a detective agency in Paris, and contacts in the Sûreté just as Samson had contacts in the CID. Occasionally they had done favours for each other – finding out whether someone in the other's country had a criminal record, or a telephone number, and information on private companies and membership clubs.

'Would you like me to call Anton?' Shandy asked.

'Ask Georgia to do it. . . . I'd like to know more about Dr Maurice and I'd like to know why my movements are being so closely watched even though I thought I'd managed to throw off any tail. Is there a constant watch on Mrs H-W's apartment block? If so, why?'

Shandy started to leave the room and then stopped. Looking directly at Samson she said, 'You saw what Georgia was wearing today?'

'Something in green, wasn't it?'

Shandy pulled a face. 'A leisure suit. Did you notice the pants? Green with a red stripe down each side and stretch cuffs at the ankles. She comes in casual gear every day.'

Every syllable of Shandy's words was sharpened with disapproval. Samson looked at her neat two-piece suit. The message was clear. Shandy didn't think Georgia was suitably dressed.

'Of course,' Shandy went on, 'if you don't object, that's fine. But it could be the thin end of the wedge. Summer's coming on. What next? Bare midriff?'

'I get the point. Okay, have a word.'

Her face softened into a smile. 'I will.'

A week-end came and went. Samson who at one time had professed deep ignorance of art found he was becoming interested in works of the old masters. He found pleasure in gazing at the windows of small art galleries near his flat and he visited the National Gallery and the Royal Academy. It was a relaxed week-end.

Monday was different. He was bombarded with calls and one of these was from Mrs Huntingdon-Winstanley.

'I've been trying to get you for ages,' she began. 'Have you only got one line to your office?'

'At present, yes. I've applied for a second line. Can I help you?'

Her tone changed from complaint to excitement. 'I've heard from him. Simon 'phoned early this morning. And I've found out where he is.'

'Where is he?'

'Don't you want to know how I found out?' She sounded peeved.

'How did you find out?'

'Well, the operator came through to ask if my number *was* my number. I knew then that it would be a long-distance call and so, instead of saying, yes, it was my number, I said, "Where is this call coming from? I must know. I refuse to take the call unless I know." A hiatus followed. Then I found myself speaking to a French operator. And what do you think? I found the call was coming from an hotel in Azay-le-Rideau. After some clicks on the line, Simon came through. What do you think he wanted?'

Samson was tired of game-playing and had to suppress an impulse to bark 'Get on with it.' 'Tell me,' he muttered.

'He wanted to talk to me! Think of it! It was more like old times before Robert came along. I think they've had a spat, a quarrel. It's happened before. They are two children.'

'Robert wasn't with him then?'

'I don't think so, but I've no doubt they'll get back together again.' Her voice became bitter. 'It's like a lovers' quarrel. If only I could wean him from Robert— '

'Did he ask after you? Your health?' Samson interrupted.

'No, and I didn't say anything. I shall leave that until he comes home and that should settle Robert one way or another. I'm sure this evil plot to poison me is all his doing. Simon wouldn't do it. He's all bluster and show but basically he's a weak man. He wouldn't have the nerve. Robert is different. He seems to have power over Simon and I wish— '

Samson again interrupted her flow. 'I'm not sure what you want of me,' he said.

'I should have thought that was obvious. I want you to go straight away to Azay-le-Rideau to find out what's going on.'

'I have an engagement list. Other clients.'

'Naturally, but much as I hate mentioning money, would five thousand pounds guarantee your services for the next two or three days?'

Her question put Samson on the spot. 'I'll see if certain arrangements can be altered without too much inconvenience to other clients,' he said. 'If they can, I'll go. If not, I shan't. What was the name of the hotel, by the way?'

'Hold on. I made a note of it somewhere.'

Samson drummed his fingers on the desk. There was a rap on the door and Georgia entered with express delivery letters. Samson signalled her to put them on the desk.

'Are you there, Mr Samson? I've found it. The hotel is the *Grande Monarche* and I even have its telephone number. 47–45–40–08. I think that's right. The person's accent wasn't *accent Tours* by a long chalk.'

'You must speak French well,' said Samson drily.

'Every civilised person speaks French well,' came the reply.

'I'll call you back later when I've had a chance to check on my other engagements, Mrs Huntingdon-Winstanley. Goodbye.' He hung up before she could delay him further.

Georgia hadn't left the room but was standing near the door, an uncharacteristically sheepish look on her face.

'You want something, Georgia?'

'Do I look all right today?'

She was wearing a cotton print dress which was one of Marks and Spencer's best-selling lines.

'You look fine.'

She smiled winsomely. 'Thanks. I wouldn't want to disgrace the old firm.'

By the time he'd finished checking his list of engagements Samson had decided to visit Azay-le-Rideau. A hired car took him to Heathrow and he caught the noon flight to Paris. At Orly he hired a two-litre Citroën and was soon speeding south. By using autoroutes he was in Azay-le-Rideau by five in the afternoon.

Chapter 12

The hotel *Grande Monarche* was near the centre of a town which had woken from winter sleep and was geared for the annual invasion of tourists keen to see its fairy-tale château. Samson parked his car in a vacant lot opposite the hotel which looked as if its architect had been influenced by old French colonial-style buildings, and went straight to the reception desk.

After booking a room for the night he enquired if there were any other English visitors staying at the hotel. He learned that a party of four from Harrogate had recently left and that a couple had booked in at midday. The receptionist nodded towards the far end of the foyer, 'Over there,' she said. Samson saw a man and woman in animated conversation. Both were middle-aged with greying hair but, like young lovers, were entirely absorbed in each other. Such was the strength of their mutual pre-occupation Samson guessed they were not married to each other.

'Is there no Mr Winstanley here?' he asked the receptionist.

'Not that I know of. Were you expecting someone of that name?'

'I thought he might be here. I need to see him. I thought he made a telephone call from this hotel early this morning.'

'Ah, I wasn't on duty then.'

The receptionist scanned the guest-list book. 'Wait a

moment,' she said. 'A Mr Winstanley booked in late last night and left early this morning.'

'Do you know where he was going?'

The receptionist shook her head. 'I don't know but my colleague might. She will be on duty at ten this evening. You could ask her.'

After thanking her for the information Samson went to his room and had a shower.

It was a balmy evening and he decided to go for a short stroll before dinner. As he wandered through the streets he became aware of the name 'Balzac'. Not only was there a street named in the author's honour but also a restaurant, and some shops had busts of Balzac in their windows. These showed a head mounted on a bull neck, a full-lipped smiling face and a big nose with wide nostrils. The brow was high, and thick hair was swept back from the forehead.

It was in a shop with a bust of Balzac on the counter that he bought a road map of the district. Apart from its possible use, he liked maps and regretted that most of his collection of maps had been destroyed by fire.

He dined at the hotel and at a few minutes after ten he went to the reception desk. A sandy-haired woman with a string of amber beads round her neck looked up as he approached.

'I booked in here earlier,' said Samson, 'and I wonder if you could help me.'

'I'll try, sir.'

'I believe a Mr Winstanley left here earlier in the day.'

'Yes, my colleague said you were enquiring about him.'

'Do you know where he was going when he left here?'

'I'm not absolutely sure. A car came to collect him and I have an idea he was going to a small château which has been converted to become some sort of a clinic. We discussed Balzac and his works while Mr Winstanley was waiting for his car and he mentioned the clinic. Like me he is an admirer of our most famous author.' The receptionist fingered her beads and her eyes lighted up. 'Mr Winstanley has visited Saché more than once. You know of Saché?'

'I'm afraid not.'

'It is less than six kilometres away and is one of the most beautiful places in the whole of Touraine. Balzac lived there in the manor-house which is now a museum in his honour. Mr Winstanley told me that the place to where he was going was being built when Balzac was in residence at Saché and the great man must have seen it. It lies on the left bank of the Indre, the river Balzac loved, and which is described so well in many of his novels. You know his books?'

'It's a gap in my education,' replied Samson sorrowfully, 'but I should like to remedy the gap. I shall visit Saché and I'd like to call at the clinic. Where exactly is it?'

'About nine or ten kilometres from here, on the road to Montbazon. As I say, the river flows through its grounds, but it isn't open for inspection. There is tight security. It is very private and recently even more private. Even trades-men are no longer allowed past the main gate but must make their deliveries . . .' She paused. A family party had entered and were making their way towards her. 'Excuse me, sir,' she said.

Samson thanked her for her help and left.

He rose early the next morning and after breakfast went out to buy some provisions. He anticipated a long, watching, waiting day. A short distance from the hotel he found a small supermarket where he purchased a bottle of Touraine red wine, a bottle of Vichy water and a tumbler. He also purchased half a kilo of tomatoes, some butter and a replacement battery for his torch.

When he travelled abroad he always took a professional kit which he called his tool-bag. It contained a small sonic tape for taking measurements, a pocket-size clock radio,

160

a mini tape-recorder, a torch, a length of yellow nylon rope, a specially assembled household tool-kit, a camera, field glasses, a microscope torch giving 40x magnification, skeleton keys, a hip flask of brandy, and a pocket calculator with additional facility for immediate translation of 10,000 words in seven different languages. This tool-bag had caused occasional problems at airport security checks but he'd always managed to convince officials of his bona fides. The bag had been searched in a security check at Heathrow on the previous day by an official who had given him a curious look when handing it back.

From the supermarket he went to a delicatessen where he bought a quiche and a large wedge of charcuterie in pastry. From a bakery he purchased a baguette. He was now set up in food and drink for the day ahead.

He had to wait a few moments before checking out of the hotel as the middle-aged English couple were just ahead of him. The man, as he moved away, turned to the woman and said, 'What's the name of your sister-in-law who lives in Manchester?'

'Christelle,' replied the woman. She took his hand. 'So many names for you to remember,' she added.

Samson smiled inwardly. His guess had been correct.

'My bill, please,' he said to the receptionist.

After checking out he went over the road to where the Citroën was parked. He was glad that it was a fine day. When venturing alone into the unknown it is usually an asset to have fair weather as an ally.

A narrow, winding road led through fertile, sparsely populated countryside. From time to time Samson saw the river to his right while, to the left, the terrain became more rugged as the road wound round an escarpment which, at one point, had bare ochre-coloured cliffs. It was shortly after a steep incline in the road, and on rounding a corner, that he saw a high stone wall ahead. He slowed down and passed a small lodge beside wrought-iron gates through which he managed to glimpse a broad curving drive leading in the direction of the river.

An indentation at the base of the cliff-face allowed him to pull off the road and stop. After locking the car doors he set off with his tool-bag to look for some place where he could climb the cliff and obtain a view from a height. Eventually he found what looked like a rough path. It was impossible to walk erect; he half-crawled and scrambled up and had to pause periodically to make sure of a firm foothold. When he arrived at the top of the cliff he was faced by dense undergrowth and his clothes were scratched as he forced his way through brambles. Twice his hands were stung by tall nettles, and low branches from overhanging trees obliged him to stoop and duck as he moved slowly forward.

In trying to keep close to the cliff top he nearly slipped on some loose shale and only saved himself from falling to almost certain death by grabbing at an exposed tree root with his free hand.

After about twenty minutes of fighting vegetation as unfriendly as the barbed wire round a prison camp he reached a small clearing. The hazardous journey was well rewarded. He had a perfect view of the château which lay at the end of the drive and was close to the winding river. The building was well preserved but unremarkable. It had three turreted towers and its façade had been constructed from the creamy stone indigenous to the area. It was a château which might have been built in the first half of the nineteenth century for occupation by a minor noble-man who had survived the Revolution and was prospering under the reign of Louis Philippe.

Samson took field glasses from his tool-bag. Once focused, these showed that some outbuildings, probably stables, had been converted into garages. A few cars were parked in a forecourt. Two men in paramilitary uniforms, and with rifles at the ready, were strolling up and down the forecourt. From their physiognomy it looked as if they were of South-East Asian origin.

After a few minutes three men and a boy came down the steps leading from the front entrance and went to a parked car. Seconds later the car moved away down the drive. Through the field glasses Samson scanned all the cars. There was no Jaguar XJ-S. He began to wonder whether his hunch that he'd find Winstanley and Mansour at the château was based on wish rather than probability. An hour passed with no more activity to be seen than the two guards wandering up and down. Samson dipped into his tool-bag and brought out the bottle of Vichy water which he had prudently packed before leaving the car.

In every assignment which involved watching and waiting there came a time when losses had to be assessed and, if necessary, cut. He decided that if there was no evidence of Winstanley and Mansour's presence by nightfall he might have to leave. He wasn't a coward, but the place was obviously well-guarded and he saw no point in risking his life by an attempt to break into the château.

The drive's entrance was obscured from view but shortly before midday a car arrived from the direction of the road. It was a large black Mercedes. A man in chauffeur's uniform got out and stood by the rear door. Within two minutes an old man wearing a straw boater emerged from the château's portico escorted by a blond-haired youth. They made their way slowly down wide stone steps to the waiting car. After closing the rear door on his passengers the chauffeur climbed into his seat and drove the Mercedes away.

No sooner had the car disappeared from view than another elderly looking man, his face heavily bandaged, came out of the château's entrance with his arm round the shoulders of a bronze-skinned youth who was wearing nothing more than a pair of trunks and sandals. The youth opened the front passenger door of a Rolls Royce Silver Shadow and helped the man inside. Then he got into the driver's seat and, after checking that his companion's seat belt was properly fastened, and fastening his own, he drove away.

The château appeared to house an all-male community and could be a rendezvous for a homosexual club as well as a clinic for cosmetic surgery.

At promptly one o'clock the guards were changed and two more men with South-East Asian features, and wearing paramilitary uniforms, were posted. For a few minutes they were joined by a huge black man wearing a gaudy uniform with gilded epaulettes. A row of medals glinted on the breast of his red tunic.

A breakthrough to reward Samson's patience came just before three in the afternoon. Robert Mansour came out of the château and made his way towards the outbuildings. His stride was purposeful. Samson grabbed his tool-bag and moved to the cliff's edge. An eighty-foot drop faced him. Below, on the road, a woman on a bicycle with a handlebar basket filled with provisions was cycling slowly in the direction of Azay-le-Rideau.

If, as he guessed, Mansour was making for the Jaguar housed in the outbuildings, there wasn't time to retrace his way through the brambles, bushes and thorn. He looked again at the drop. The cliff-face wasn't sheer but it was too steep for safe descent. Hurriedly he took the length of nylon rope from the tool-bag, tied one end round the trunk of an oak tree and threw the loose part over the cliff-face. It ended about fifteen feet short of the road.

He looped the straps of the tool-bag round his shoulders to make a satchel.

The Jaguar was being backed out of a garage.

Hauling up the rope he swiftly tied the loose end round his waist, knotting it securely.

The Jaguar was moving towards the drive's entrance.

Samson took a deep breath, gripped the rope firmly and turned his back on the château. He was now ready for his first ever attempt at abseiling.

On the descent he barked his knees, burned the palms of his hands and almost tipped over sideways. When he reached the end of the rope's length he untied the knot and dropped. His fall was the equivalent of dropping from the roof of a two-storey house but before releasing the knot he had turned to face the road so that he could view the ground as it rushed up at him.

The impact was harsher than he had expected and, although he buckled at the knees on contact, it knocked the breath from his body. He rolled forward like a parachutist. Apart from jarring his spine and bruising a shoulder, and apart from painful knees and burning hands, he was all right.

He began running towards his car.

He managed to unlock the door, throw the tool-bag on to the back seat, and climb inside a split second before the Jaguar rounded a corner. He knew then that luck was on his side. Mansour could have travelled in the opposite direction, towards Azay-le-Rideau, and have disappeared without trace.

Samson switched on the engine but frustratingly couldn't set off in hot pursuit. He cursed the Citroën's leisurely rising from its aerodynamic haunches. If you want a getaway car, he thought, never choose a Citroën.

But when the car had completed its camel-like elevation it went swifter than the fiercest khamsin sweeping across the desert.

Within three minutes he was on the tail of the Jaguar. He waited until both cars were past a farmhouse and then moved out to overtake. It was a risky manoeuvre because he was overtaking blind on a corner but the risk came off and as he passed the other car he swung the wheel and hit the Jaguar's front wheel arch.

Able to control the Citroën because he had anticipated the swerve from collision he fared better than Mansour who, taken unawares, skidded to the side of the road and came to a halt. Samson jammed on his brakes and waited. He knew that if he got out of his car to confront Mansour, the other, on seeing who it was, might drive off, but if he stayed put and kept his head down, the angry Mansour would leave his car and come to him.

He was right. In the rear-view mirror he saw Mansour leap out of the stalled Jaguar and come running towards him. The enemy was out in the open. It was time to move. Samson unfastened his door just before Mansour reached the Citroën, leapt out, and head-butted the other man hard in the stomach.

Chapter 13

A car passed close by as Samson frog-marched Mansour towards a clump of bushes. He glimpsed the startled face of a woman driver before the car accelerated away.

Once behind the bushes and screened from the road Samson released his grip. 'I'd like a little talk with you,' he said.

'You bastard!'

'Many a true word spoken in spite,' Samson replied. 'First of all, what goes on at that so-called clinic?'

'You'll get nothing from me.'

The words had the ring of bravado but Mansour's eyes were darting around looking for a means of escape from the man who had backed him up against the bushes.

'What goes on at that so-called clinic?'

'It was you that did me over in the underground car-park that day, wasn't it?'

'Yes. I can get much nastier than that. I don't like doing it, but I can get extremely nasty.'

Mansour seemed to shrink physically. He was almost as tall as his adversary but he looked much smaller. 'I don't know what you want,' he said. 'The clinic is just a place where rich people come for treatment. It's all above board. It's licensed by the authorities.'

'What sort of treatment?'

'Home improvements. Nose jobs, face lifts, that sort of thing.' Mansour gave a timid smile. 'I don't know what all this is about. I think you've made a mistake. Everything's above board, like I say.'

'The boys and young men. Do they need face lifts?'
The timid smile vanished. 'What's this? A moral crusade? They're all willing and well paid. Very well paid, I can tell you.'

'You can tell me because you recruited them. That's your function, isn't it? That's where you fit in.'

'What if it is? It's no business of yours.'

Mansour's voice was becoming stronger and he pointedly brushed the sleeve of his coat where it had been gripped by Samson.

'Indecent acts with minors is an offence in France,' said Samson.

'The acts have to be proved, don't they?'

'Not necessarily. As I understand it, under French law the onus is on the defendant to show he is guiltless.'

'I don't know about that but, like I say, the guys are well paid and willing. I don't see what it matters to you. Okay, I'm gay, Simon's gay, so what? Maybe there are gays at the clinic, so what? If that jealous old bitch doesn't like it, that's just too bad. Who the hell could fancy her anyway?'

'She could be fancied for her money.'

Mansour looked down at the ground but not before Samson had seen the spark of acquisitiveness lighten soft brown eyes.

'All right, so she has a lot of loot, but you can't take it with you, can you?'

'No,' Samson agreed. 'She can't take her money with her but she can leave everything to charity.'

Mansour looked up. 'That's where you're wrong, dead wrong,' he said triumphantly. 'The law says that the widow, or widower, in this case Simon, is entitled to a fair whack.'

'In this case,' replied Samson quietly, 'not Simon.'

Mansour's moment of confidence, inspired by a slight knowledge of English inheritance law, began to seep out of him. 'What do you mean?'

168

'I mean that your employers are not man and wife. That's what I mean.'

Samson was gambling that Mansour wouldn't know about a marriage in the Seychelles.

Mansour opened his mouth and closed it without speaking.

'They never have been married,' Samson went on. 'If they have, you tell me where they were married and when.'

'I wouldn't know about a thing like that. Why the hell should Simon want to talk about how a disaster began?'

'Ask him to show you his marriage certificate. I promise you he won't be able to.'

Doubt spread over Mansour's handsome features. 'You're lying,' he said, but the accusation wasn't spoken with conviction.

'I've got no reason to lie. She made him change his name to hers because she wanted it to be thought that they were married and because his proper name was too common for her liking.'

'That bit figures,' muttered Mansour.

'Until you came along she had a reasonable relationship with her husband. Not good, but reasonable. Tolerable.'

'Well, I'm not clearing out if that's what she wants.'

'She could dismiss you.'

'Could she?' Mansour sneered. 'I've got enough dirt on her precious Simon to crucify him. He has some funny tastes, very funny.'

'Blackmail?'

'If you like. I can fight nasty too.'

'I could break your neck,' said Samson calmly, 'and leave your body here to rot. No one would trace it to me. Your friend Hawkey isn't the only one who can do a tidy job.'

Mansour's face registered alarm. 'What do you know about him?'

'Doesn't he want his features professionally rearranged,

169

and haven't you and Simon been acting as fixers?'

'I don't know what you're talking about.'

'You must have mixed with a queer crowd when you were a rent-boy. The criminal fraternity have their queers. It's not all dolls dripping furs and dressed to over-kill with jewellery.' Samson paused. 'But then,' he added reflectively, 'every fraternity has its queers. No, I'm not a moral crusader. I'm just a humble private investigator hired to find out what goes on when you and your boss visit France. Now I know. While Simon collects books and indulges his tastes on the side, you search for talent and fix cosmetic operations for one or two rich crooks. You must make quite a bit on commission. But don't count on expectations from Simon. He hasn't any, I can assure you.'

'But he must have or else why should he— '

Mansour broke off suddenly like someone who knows that some truths, if allowed to escape, can blow up in one's face.

'Why should he – what?' asked Samson.

'Nothing.'

'Were you going to say – "Why should he be poisoning her if he didn't expect to inherit something by operation of the law, if not by her will?"'

Mansour looked aghast. 'What do you know?'

'I know enough to get you both sent down for a long stretch. Face creams, lipstick and eye make-up have been analysed.'

'Christ!'

'If that is a plea to our Saviour,' said Samson drily, 'I think even his compassion would be put under pressure. You are a shit, Mansour. Bum-boy, ponce and shit.'

Mansour's eyes flared and he made a movement towards Samson.

'Don't try to take me on,' said the detective, 'you would regret it for the rest of a very, very short life.'

In the silence which followed the song of a blackbird

could be heard. It was drowned by the harsh and ugly exhaust note of a Vespa approaching from the direction of Montbazon. Nearby, the branches of a tall aspen tree quivered in a breeze which failed to ruffle the bushes where Samson and Robert Mansour were fighting a verbal duel. The sound of the Vespa was fading in the distance when Mansour broke the silence.

'It's nothing to do with me,' he said. 'It was Simon's idea and Maurice owed him a favour.'

'I'd like to know more about Dr Maurice. Tell me about him.'

'He's a plastic surgeon. The best.'

'He was once married to a French woman, I believe.'

Mansour raised finely arched eyebrows. 'You do know a lot.'

'It's my business.'

'You're right. They divorced when she realised he had other tastes.'

'What favour did he owe?'

Mansour shuffled his feet like someone who has stayed too long on the same spot and wants to move, but is unable.

'They got to know each other through old books. Paul Maurice is a collector too and Simon sussed out his other interest.'

'So they shared, did they?'

'Shared?'

'Shared both their interests?'

For the first time Mansour looked embarrassed. 'You could say that.'

'You filled a sandwich, so to speak.'

'For Christ's sake!'

'Where did Dr Maurice come from? He's not English, is he?'

'Montreal, I think. I think he qualified there. He's a French Canadian.'

'And the poison was Simon's idea entirely?'

'Right. Absolutely right. . . . Were you on the level about them not being married?'

'Absolutely. I checked it out. It's my business.'

'I just don't see the point then.'

'The point,' said Samson, 'is that they live in one of the most expensive parts of London and the apartment is worth at least one million pounds.'

'What's that got to do with it?'

Samson had already lied about his knowledge of the marriage and he lied again when he said, 'I've checked with the Land Registry. The apartment is owned by them in their joint names as joint tenants. This means that whoever survives the other takes the whole. If Mrs Huntingdon-Winstanley dies first Mr Winstanley will automatically be entitled to ownership of the whole premises.'

'So that's what he's on to.'

'Yes.'

'She knows this, does she?'

'She does now. He won't get anything. She's having treatment for the poisoning and has seen her lawyer about deception and fraud. It'll be a court case. The Land Registry entry will be cancelled and she'll be registered as sole owner.'

'It's . . .' Mansour was lost for words.

'Downright immoral,' supplied Samson with an ironic smile.

'I knew he was on to something, but he wouldn't tell me. I knew there was something else cooking. We had a row about it the night before last. I'd smelled something fishy. But I didn't know they weren't married and he was expecting the value of the apartment.'

'Now you do know. But that'll be changed when her lawyer gets to work and then there'll be nothing. Nothing at all.'

Another silence fell which Samson broke by saying, 'Where were you going when I stopped you?'

172

'Nowhere. Just out for a spin.'

'A breath of fresh air?'

'That's right.'

'I should think you needed it,' said Samson. 'It must pollute the air having armed guards around the place.'

'It does. And they're all martial arts experts. You may think you're tough but you wouldn't stand a chance against those guys. They're killers.'

'Why are they there? What needs guarding?'

'Nothing yet.'

'What do you mean?'

A shifty look came to Mansour's eyes and he glanced around as if fearful of being overheard. 'I don't see why I shouldn't tell you. I know something. I'm not supposed to know it, but I do. The place is afloat with rumours but I got it from the horse's mouth.' He laughed. 'Pillow talk in the stable, in a manner of speaking. Some filthy rich guy from a banana republic in Africa is expected and he's paranoiac about security and anyone getting hold of the news. He wants a nick here and there to take off a few years and if it's done well it could provide a new identity. Dead straight, you see. The rest of us have to be out of the place by midnight tonight.' Mansour widened his eyes theatrically. 'It's top, top secret! And I'm telling you for free. I'll tell you something else. If you've had any aggravation, put it down to the goons on His Excellency's payroll and interested governments. Like I say, he's paranoiac and doesn't want anyone nosing around.'

To Samson, some unexplained happenings began to slot into place.

'Governments are involved?'

'I've said enough. I'm not saying any more.'

'A precious ornament was smashed in my flat.'

'I haven't a clue about that.'

Samson's acuity to lie-detection was highly tuned. He felt sure Mansour wasn't lying.

In the far distance a police siren wailed.

'Is that for us?' asked Mansour.

'It could be. I was seen assisting you here.'

'I don't want police trouble. Do you?'

'No,' said Samson.

'It was just a friendly argument. Right? No hard feelings. No charges. No damage done.'

The wailing siren was very close and they could hear the sound of a car slowing down.

'It pains me to join you in deceiving the police,' said Samson, 'but it's in my interests as well as yours. Just one other thing. As of now you're fired from the service of the Winstanleys. You will stay away from Mrs Huntingdon-Winstanley and if I find that you've caused any more trouble I shall inflict my presence on you in a most harmful way.'

'You can't fire me.'

'I just have.'

'I was thinking of leaving anyway. Simon's getting too possessive and the old bird is tough. She could hang on for a while yet.'

Together they emerged from behind the bushes.

It was a few minutes before they managed to convince the police that they had no quarrel, and that what the woman driver had witnessed was merely a bit of horse-play. But they succeeded and each got into his own car, Mansour to continue a journey to an unknown destination and Samson to head for Orly Airport.

At Tours, partly due to a road-works diversion, and partly to bad signposting, Samson found himself travelling along the north bank of the Loire when he should have been on the Autoroute L'Aquitaine a few miles to the west. He stopped at a lay-by just past Amboise and studied a map. Having seen that he was still on a direct route to Orléans and thence to Paris he decided to make a break for a late lunch.

Water scenes – rivers, lakes, harbours – never failed to give him pleasure and as he made inroads into the provisions bought earlier in the day he gazed at fast-running brownish waters and at a tree-covered island in the centre of this broad reach of river. The break provided relaxation after the events of the day. The thought that he might be getting too old for this sort of investigative exercise briefly entered his mind and was as briefly dismissed. He dreaded the idea of retirement and the downward spiral into old age which slowly drags the strongest constitution into a pit of eternal oblivion.

The thought of old age brought with it the memory of Mrs Huntingdon-Winstanley's raddled face with its tired and deeply fissured skin. How would she react to the information, if Mansour was to be believed, that her husband was deliberately poisoning her?

It was difficult to believe that Brightwell's death, the tampering with the brakes of his own car, the assault in a dark alleyway, and the broken goblet were all connected and measures to prevent a too close enquiry into the whereabouts of some VIP from a banana republic. But if not, what was the explanation?

He threw the remains of his meal on to the river bank for the benefit of any birds in the vicinity and was rewarded by the prompt attention of a hedge sparrow. 'Share and share alike' he said aloud as he climbed back into the Citroën.

'Paris, here we come,' he said, again aloud. Lonely people often speak to themselves. It is not necessarily a sign of deteriorating faculties, or so he assured himself when he heard the sound of his own voice.

It was on the concourse at Orly Airport, after he had returned the hired car, that a man in grey suit and red tie approached him. Speaking in a mid-Atlantic accent he said, 'Mr Samson?'

'Yes.'

175

'I hope your investigations have been completed.'

'Who are you?'

'That doesn't matter. By accident you've become a small fish swimming in someone's private pool, a pool which contains dangerous predators. You've been lucky so far. Don't push your luck. And if a breath of what you might know should waft towards the media, the predators might get angry and not be content with warnings. I hope you get me.'

A woman carrying a suitcase almost bumped into them. 'So heavy,' she gasped in French. And then, looking at the two men, 'If either of you were gentlemen you'd offer to give me a hand.'

Samson said, 'My flight has already been called.'

The other man said, 'There are porters for that job. Get one.'

The woman picked up her suitcase. 'Foreigners have no manners,' she said.

The diversion gave Samson a chance to assess the situation.

'There are political overtones?' he asked.

'Maybe.'

'I'm not concerned with balances of power in the Third World or whether certain men might need to disappear only to emerge with a new face and possibly a new identity.'

The anonymous man gave a taut-lipped smile. 'Good. I'm glad.' With that he walked away and disappeared behind a crowd of schoolchildren.

By the time he reached his flat Samson was ready for sleep and he went straight to bed. But his mind was over-active and suddenly he became wide awake. It was three in the morning before he finally fell asleep.

Chapter 14

The following day he arrived late at his office.

Georgia greeted him with, 'There's a whole lot of people wanting you to call them.'

'Give me five minutes and then get me Mrs Huntingdon-Winstanley.'

He walked through Shandy's room. 'How was France?' she asked. 'You haven't got much of a holiday tan.'

He gave her a sour look and went on his way.

'Sorry,' she called after him. 'It was just a joke.'

'Mrs Huntingdon-Winstanley?'

A feeble voice said, 'Who is it?'

'John Samson here.'

'You're back?'

'Yes, and I'd like to see you.'

A long pause. 'I'm not feeling too well. I've been in bed since I last spoke to you.'

'May I come and see you? I have something to say which you should know.'

'Did you find them?'

'Yes.'

'It isn't Simon, is it?'

'I'd like to come and talk with you.'

Another long pause.

'I don't know whether I can receive you. I'm in bed.'

'I think I should see you.'

'Oh, very well. But I shan't be able to open the fire-escape door.'

'That doesn't matter. I'll come in the conventional way. I shall be busy the rest of this morning but would it be all right if I come about three in the afternoon?'

'Did you speak to Simon?'

'No, but I spoke to Robert.'

'I hope he didn't get round you. He's a born liar, you know.'

'If I come this afternoon, would that be convenient?'

'I'll tell Jennifer to expect you.'

Samson had half expected his client to have made the effort to dress and receive him in the sitting room. But the maid, looking anxious, said, 'She'll see you in her bedroom. I wish, sir, you could persuade her to see a doctor. She's very poorly.' As they moved towards the stairs, she continued, 'I don't know what's the matter with her. I think she's gone a bit peculiar. She won't show her face.'

'How do you mean?'

'She's got a silk scarf which she wears over her face. Like a bandit or a bank robber. You can only see her eyes. It is most peculiar, sir.'

The maid's eyes seemed to swim in the gold-fish bowls of her spectacle lenses.

'For two pins I'd hand in my notice,' she said, 'but I don't like leaving a sinking ship, if you know what I mean.'

Samson who had once during his naval career eagerly left such a ship without the slightest qualm said, 'I know what you mean but try to stick it out. She needs you.'

The maid paused by the bedroom door and gave a diffident knock. 'He's here, ma'am,' she called out.

A thin voice replied, 'Let him in.'

The maid opened the door. 'You can go in, sir,' she said and Samson entered the room not unlike a reluctant lion being pushed into the circus ring.

Mrs Huntingdon-Winstanley was sitting up in her copious bed with a pink shawl draped over her shoulders. Above a red silk scarf her eyes glittered beneath ashen pale forehead and the henna-chestnut wig.

The maid quietly closed the door.

Curtains were drawn over the windows and the pinkness of the room's decor was illuminated by table lamps and an overhead light. An overpowering odour of 4711 eau de cologne gave a sickly sweetness to the stuffy atmosphere.

'Take a seat, Mr Samson.'

Samson picked up a wide stool covered in green and pink striped draylon and brought it to the bedside.

'That's quite close enough,' said Mrs Huntingdon-Winstanley, her voice slightly distorted and muffled by the scarf. 'Tell me everything.'

Samson began with his flight to Orly and was listened to in attentive silence until he came to the point in his narrative where he frog-marched Robert Mansour into a secluded spot behind bushes.

'I hope you hurt him,' said Mrs Huntingdon-Winstanley viciously.

Samson spoke of the clinic and how it was obviously a place where cosmetic surgery was performed but it also was a rendezvous for homosexuals.

'I thought it would be something like that,' she said, 'but how do you know there weren't women in the place? Surgery of that sort requires nursing care.' And then, answering her own question, 'I expect they were all male nurses.'

To Samson's surprise tears filled her eyes. She fumbled for a tissue under her pillow and wiped her eyes. 'Please continue,' she said.

'I took a gamble. To discourage him I said that you and Mr Winstanley weren't married and there could be no financial expectations.'

'You had absolutely no right to say we weren't married,' she said angrily.

'But you aren't married, are you?'

Her eyes held him in a fixed stare. 'How dare you suggest that Simon and I aren't married!'

'This is what makes me dare,' said Samson and, before she could stop him, he had reached out and snatched the scarf from her face.

On withered cheeks a strong growth of silver-grey stubble glinted in the harsh electric light.

The silence which followed was no less electric.

It was broken by the man whom Samson would always think of as 'Mrs H-W'. 'How did you know? Was it my voice?'

'Not really. Quite a few women have deep voices. But I was surprised by the fact that you were so against orthodox medicine. As a former nurse you would know the risks you were taking by not seeking proper medical attention. But you were deterred by fear of discovery. A doctor would have examined you and discovered you were male. This same fear of discovery made you accuse me of interfering with you the day you fainted. You were afraid I might have discovered your secret while you were unconscious.'

'On such slight foundations you knew about me?'

'Yes.'

He didn't add that there had been other indicators. He didn't say he had wondered if she was some sort of phoney when, at their first meeting, she'd leaned forward, elbows on table and chin cupped in hands. Nor did he say that when he had called on her and she had been dressed to kill, and had later simpered that she admired a man who was a real man, he had sensed a wrongness. Her dress and words although feminine in essence were somehow false. He had sensed a deceit beyond the common deceit of flattery. To these random suspicions had been added the memory of straightening her wig after she had fainted at the sight of red and white carnations. He had seen a scalp thinly covered in wispy white hair. At the time he had assumed that like some very elderly women she had suffered a natural hair loss but later it was another factor adding to his suspicion that her deceit involved gender. Finally, he had realised that the shaving soap and razor might not have been used for female depilation.

'I suppose I should have expected a detective like you to find out my little secret,' she said.

'I haven't found out who sent you the carnations.'

'That was Robert, of course. I remembered later how once, when he first came to us and I hadn't learned of his true nature, I told him about my superstitions. It was a wicked thing for him to do, but he is a wicked man.'

She indicated a tray by the bedside table on which was a bottle of sparkling spring water and a crystal tumbler. 'Pour me a glass of water, would you?'

After she had taken a few sips she said, 'Now you can continue.'

Samson was glad of the break to pour out water for her. It gave him the opportunity to accustom himself to the sight of the strange figure who looked like a pensioner hermaphrodite.

'I tackled Mansour about the poisoned cosmetics,' he said.

'And he accused Simon, I'm sure.'

'He did.'

'The rat. It was probably something he and Dr Maurice cooked up together. I should be killed and any suspicion would fall on Simon if the true cause of death was discovered. But by that time Robert would have milked Simon for what he could get from my estate. . . . Well, what do you think?'

'It's a possibility.'

'Poor Simon. He's such a dupe and he thinks he's so clever. He does have some intellectual ability, I admit. He's by no means unlettered, as I've said before. But the difference between him and Robert is the difference

181

between a highbrow fool and a streetwise rogue.' She paused for breath and began to tremble. Her crabbed hand reached for the region of her stomach. 'Quick,' she whispered. 'One of those pills.' She nodded towards a bottle of white tablets. 'It's the colic,' she said, 'brought on by that terrible stuff.'

As she washed down two tablets with water Samson examined the bottle. It had come from a homeopathic pharmacy and the tablets were recommended for heartburn and indigestion.

'Do these do any good?' he asked.

'Not much. Morphia is really the only remedy for acute colic, but that makes one feel sick, and anyway I can only get morphia on prescription.'

'You really should let a doctor see you.'

She handed him the empty glass. 'A little more, please.'

When he gave her the refilled glass he said, 'Isn't it time the eighth deadly sin was put aside?'

She looked at the crumpled red scarf lying on the bedspread. 'Perhaps it is. After all, you have stripped me of the last of my vanity.'

'Let me call a doctor.'

'No. Not yet. I still want to fight this my own way. The pain is easing. Go on. What else was said when you hijacked Robert?'

Samson didn't see any point in telling her about his encounter with the anonymous man at Orly Airport or the probability that the clinic was used as a place for cosmetic or plastic surgery on people who had every reason to shun the media spotlight. Nor did there seem any reason to mention the threats to his own personal safety.

He said, 'I took the liberty of dismissing Mansour from your service.'

'You did? Well done! If I hadn't been so afraid of losing Simon I would . . . Oh, it doesn't matter.'

Samson relieved her of the glass of water.

'Would you mind plumping up my pillows for me, Mr Samson?'

With an effort she leaned forward and Samson, lightly bemused by his own acquiescence, pulled and patted the pillows.

'That's better,' she sighed as she settled back. 'I suppose I couldn't tempt you to take on employment with me?'

'You could not. Now I'd like to ask you something. Didn't Mansour realise that you were male?'

'He didn't. I completely fooled him. That delighted me. Another boost to my vanity.'

'But Simon could have told him.'

'Why should he? It wasn't in his interests.'

Samson nodded. 'I see. And now will you tell me the truth?'

'The truth,' she asked sharply. 'What truth?'

'The truth about yourself, about your background.'

Her manner changed and something like a twinkle came to her eyes. 'Shall I?'

'No more games, please,' he said warningly. 'The truth.'

'All right. I don't see why not. You know too much already. . . . The truth is that my father was a butler and my mother a cook to someone in the landed gentry. He and his family had one of the longest entries in Burke's. Everything had to be done very correctly and I grew up in an atmosphere of gracious living which appealed to me.

'A regular visitor was a maiden lady of somewhat eccentric disposition who took a liking to me. Everyone else was a little afraid of her but we got on like a house on fire. She even once asked me if I'd like to come and look after her. I was only fifteen at the time and didn't take it seriously. I thought it was just an eccentricity. My father died when I was twenty-two and I took over his job as butler. And then the war came. I managed to avoid service for quite a while but eventually got called up. I went into the RAMC and in due course became a medical orderly.... Are you still with me?'

Samson nodded.

'You weren't looking at me and seemed half asleep.'

'I was listening intently. You became a medical orderly. And then?'

'It was during this period that I realised I was a woman in a man's body. I'd had intimations many times before but now I knew it. I couldn't go back to butlering. And so, after the war ended I trained as a nurse, a male nurse. It was after I'd been a couple of years at an NHS hospital that the eccentric old lady entered my life again. Once more she asked if I'd look after her. I agreed. From that time the course of my life was set.

'She was something of a recluse and we spent a lot of time together. In the mornings she would study the *Financial Times*. She was an expert in the stock market; she knew exactly when to buy and when to sell. In the evenings we would either play cards or Spillikins. She loved Spillikins. And romantic novels too, as I do. And she loved furs. She would wear a different fur stole every day, even in summer. Now it so happened that an occasional visitor to the house was a nephew called Simon. She knew he was only after her money but she tolerated him. The poor dear was suffering. Her vision was going and she refused to see a doctor. When eventually she did consent to treatment it was too late. The optic nerve had been destroyed. Glaucoma. This meant she could no longer play Spillikins or read. She was blind. This threw extra work on to me. I had to read through prices of stocks and shares every day and her memory was so good she would know if any particular share had lost or gained a point from the previous day. Playing the stock market became her main passion. She would be on the 'phone to her broker at least two or three times each day. . . . All this is rather exhausting. Are you sure you want to hear any more?'

'If it doesn't tire you too much.'

'It does tire me, but I'll tell you. . . . The upshot was that I could dress as I wished, her being blind, you see. I began to dress as a woman, only changing if I knew a visitor was expected. Then one day Simon called unexpectedly and caught me. To my amazement he said I made a wonderfully attractive woman and he promised to keep my secret. And then my patron died. She left the whole of her estate, which was considerable, to me. There was only one condition. To inherit I had to change my name to hers. I was born with Briggs as a surname. I didn't object to the condition. Simon was furious about the will and wanted to contest it but was advised against doing so. Anyway, he proved to be a good loser and he began courting me. . . . Do I have to go on? You can guess the rest.'

'Thank you for telling me.'

'It's all water under the bridge now. But when my age began to show he grew restless and had some little affairs, but he would always come back to me. He never left me in spirit, if you understand me. That is, until Robert came along to seduce him.'

A silence fell. Samson got ready to leave. He stood up and put the green and pink striped stool back in its original position.

'You've been a great help to me, Mr Samson.'

'Of some help, I hope.'

'I shall see to it that your fee is paid in full. I'll telephone my accountant as soon as you've gone.' She paused. 'I shan't be sorry to get rid of this,' she said, removing her wig and placing it on the bedspread. 'It was getting too loose. I think my scalp must be shrinking.'

'You've decided to "come out" have you?'

185

'Ha! I like that! Yes, I'm coming out of the closet.' She was about to say something else but paused. There were sounds outside the room. The maid's voice could be heard and it seemed to be raised in protest. A moment later the door burst open and Winstanley strode in.

Chapter 15

Winstanley stopped dead when he saw Samson, the wig on the bedspread and the ghostly face of the man who had passed as his wife.

The three men looked at one another.

Then Winstanley moved forward towards the bed and a moment later was holding the woman who was a man in his arms. Her arms circled his shoulders. It was like a reunion of lovers. No word was spoken.

Samson silently left the room.

Outside, the maid was waiting, timorous expectancy on her face.

'Leave them alone,' he said and he went on his way.

Back at his office Georgia greeted him with, 'Shandy wants to speak to you, Mr Samson. She asked me to tell you as soon as you came in. It's important.'

He went to his room and Shandy joined him. 'I've had Anton on the 'phone from Paris,' she said. 'He sounded pretty nervous. I think he was afraid the line was being tapped.'

Samson gazed at her benignly. 'What's all the fuss about? That doesn't sound like Anton.'

'He's got an "in" with some guy at their Ministry of Foreign Affairs and apparently it's all very hush-hush and top secret. They don't want another Bokassa scandal. There's some deal going on with a central African republic which was once a French colony. It's a deal involving mineral rights, aircraft and armaments. Part of the deal involves a change of identity of their first minister. The British government is in on the act. It all has to be kept very secret in case the Americans get wind of the deal and screw it up. Anton's advice to you is to stay completely clear of the whole thing.'

Samson frowned. 'In that case I wonder why the clinic hasn't been closed down before now.'

'I believe it has. At least, pro tem. The African is scheduled to arrive at any time. Did you see a helicopter pad?'

Samson shook his head.

'Apparently there's one just behind the château. Incidentally there's no reference to a Dr Maurice in the French Medical Directory.'

For a few moments Samson was sunk in thought. And then, 'What Anton says about HM Government being involved could explain a lot including the break-in at Mrs Brightwell's house, watch being kept on Mrs H-W's block and the interest the police took in watching Georgia, not that they'd have known why they were ordered to watch.' And, as he spoke, he remembered the curious look he had received from the security official at Heathrow. His movements abroad were being noted and, no doubt, passed on to someone in France.

'What about the break-in at your flat?' Shandy asked.

'I think that was Mansour trying to warn me off. He probably got one of his criminal friends to break in or, as we've said before, it could just have been some street noise which shattered the goblet. We'll probably never know. As for the brake failures, I think he may have been behind those too. He had the right contacts, Winstanley had the money, and neither wanted Brightwell or me to foul up the scene.'

'Do you think Winstanley knew what was in the cosmetics? It wasn't just Mansour?'

'That's another thing we'll probably never know,' he said. He then went on to tell her what had transpired that afternoon. 'It was quite a touching reunion,' he concluded, 'or it would have been if I didn't suspect Winstanley had gritted his teeth, closed his eyes, and gone into an act. He knew that if he behaved like that there would be nothing I could do except leave. Mrs H-W – I still have to call her/him that – would stick by whatever he said, not what I might say.' He stretched his legs under the desk, leaned back and stretched his arms.

'Tired?' asked Shandy.

'Mrs H-W would tell you that a *gentleman* is *never* tired. But yes, I'm tired. It's an early night tonight.'

Shandy moved forward and picked up a small pile of papers on the side of the desk. 'I'll sort these out,' she said, 'and deal with what I can. You go home.'

He gave a wry smile. 'Home? What's that?'

'Oh, for God's sake! Don't give me the *Sonata Pathétique*.'

His smile broadened. 'That's what I like about you. Qualities of sympathy and tact.'

'I'll ignore that. Do you think Mrs H-W modelled herself on the eccentric recluse?'

'That's another thing I like about you. You're quick on the uptake!'

Two days later in the morning mail there was a note on pink deckel-edged writing paper with address heavily embossed in green. The note said:

Dear John,
Thank you so much for all you did to help me. I shall be forever grateful.
    Yours sincerely,
    CYRIL

'Hmm, first name terms,' said Shandy when Samson handed her the note, 'that's an accolade.'

'Not only first names, but the true name. Goodbye Sybil: hello, Cyril.'

'Another file to be marked "Closed" and put away.'

Later that morning Samson received a call from Paris. After replacing the handset he went to Shandy's room. 'The file on the Winstanley case isn't quite closed. There's a postscript. I've just had a call from Anton. Robert Mansour was found dead of a broken neck in an alleyway at the back of Montmartre. A witness says someone of oriental appearance was running away from the scene. There are no other witnesses and an arrest is unlikely.'

Shandy brushed back her wayward lock of hair. 'Maybe he knew too much about the African connection with the clinic and had to be silenced.'

'Could be.'

'Will you tell Cyril?'

'No. My professional job is finished and I've no wish to extend the relationship.'

Shandy pondered for a moment. 'Now that he's decided to reverse roles,' she said, 'and go back to square one, the square of his true gender, I wonder if he'll get medical treatment for the poisoning?'

'He'd be a fool not to,' said Samson. 'See you later.'

Shandy and her husband enjoyed their holiday in Florence and on the day visit to Venice she purchased another Murano glass goblet. When she gave it to Samson he thanked her and said, 'I shall treasure it, but it won't be the same.'

'Substitutes never are, but they can grow on you.'

It was three months, almost to the day after he had last seen Cyril Huntingdon-Winstanley, that Samson received a picture postcard from the Seychelles.

I'm having a wonderful time during my convalescence here. Hope we can meet again on my return. I'll be looking forward to it. Love, CYRIL.

190

He showed the card to Shandy without comment.

She laughed, patted her hair with elegantly extended fingers, and in mincing tones said, 'Like a game of Spillikins, darling?'

Samson gave one of his heaviest sighs. 'All my life I've dreamed of the day when I'd get a postcard sent with love from someone incredibly rich. Why, when it finally arrives, does it have to be from a man?'